FAULKNER & FRIENDS

A novel
by

Vicki Salloum

1322 Joseph Street
New Orleans, LA 70115
(504) 897-6581
vwsalhol@aol.com

Published by Underground Voices
www.undergroundvoices.com
Editor contact: Cetywa Powell

ISBN: 978-0-9904331-0-1

Printed in the United States of America.

For my family, Mimi and Jo-Jo,
Jan and Richard

Hold your face up to the Light,
even though for the moment you do not see.
--Bill Wilson

CONTENTS

I. the grand opening

Annie Ajami stepped out of the doorway on the morning of her grand opening. With hands inside her pockets, she gazed across Magazine Street at the lonely stretch of buildings rising from the solitude of the icy pavement.

She imagined within an hour couples peering through the barred windows of Sal's Antiques and Art Emporium (a junk shop) or grabbing a frittata at Maya's Latin Fusion or a hot brandy at the Dollar Bar before wandering to her shop to view through her picture window the magnificent display of books over the bars jutting up like arrows. And because she was freezing — chilled down to her bones — she turned to go inside.

She opened the door as if she were the first customer gazing in on her creation: the novels on shelves, the crushed blue velvet sofa in the center of the room with an armchair next to it, the end table and honeysuckle-scented irises in the vase where she'd placed it, her desk to the left of the entranceway where she would ring up her purchases. She made her way out, preparing to greet her customers.

A squat fellow with slanting eyes, cap down low over his skull, scratched his dick as he roamed past, bound for the Discount Mart or Vito's Lounge or maybe even Downtown. Another with rheumy eyes, mottled skin, and wrinkled forehead shivered as he approached in light-brown greasy pants before stumbling over a sidewalk crack, his breath like plumes of smoke commingling with the frigid air. He fell against a lamppost, wrapped his arm about it, then staggered to the end of the block and turned a corner toward the river.

A man and woman approached, the man gripping a six-pack. He was ranting at the woman. She could imagine him ripping off a can and knocking her to the ground and stuffing it in her mouth, that's how frightening his tone of voice. Annie strained to catch his words but the wail of a siren obliterated all sound so that she was forced to merely watch, surmise what he was getting so pissed about from the look on his beet-red face.

It was a little past ten o'clock. She found herself alone. She turned to go inside, to the place that was her 'home' now. And through it all, despite what she'd seen and heard, this day — December 27, 2003 — would live in her heart forever. She was living the life of dreams, unstained by pretense or false effort or rebuff or humiliation. And if this turned out to be a mistake, this dream come true for her, she'd go to her grave knowing that she never understood the world or God's intention for her, knowing she was living the unavoidable truth she had totally and completely failed.

But this was not what she wanted to believe. She had no reason to believe that now. How could something so desperately wanted, possibly be bad? Earlier, before stepping out, she'd surveyed her books, not a false one in the lot, not one of poor content or value put on the shelf merely to sell. Here, in the Irish Channel, at 2120 Magazine Street, she imagined who would buy them. Perhaps a great writer might wander in and find a classic no longer in print and be thrilled with his discovery and hang out for the rest of his life. Or a youth still in school might walk into her shop, find a world he couldn't live without, become a book reviewer or scholar or fiction writer or poet. She might even find a friend. She rubbed her hands for warmth, slipped on a pair of gloves, made her way out, and stood beside the door. An old woman and two boys approached.

*

Nehemiah Casimier held his Grandma's hand, his cousin walking behind him. They had come from the dead-end street looking for a way out of the freezing chill. He was careful as he stepped, making sure Grandma Zella didn't trip. She'd broken her arm in a fall over a cracked sidewalk not that many months ago. Her arm had since healed but she was walking with a pronounced waddle, her arthritis kicking in, as she trudged straight ahead, ignoring him and Delfeayo. A brown scarf looped about her neck and her shoes were tattered slippers. She wore socks, blood-red lipstick. He and Feayo had on jeans and woolen shirts, socks and tennis shoes. It couldn't be more than 15°F, yet neither of them wore jackets. It was fiercely cold; he squeezed his collar and with the other hand held Grandma. Unexpectedly, she let go.

She took off for the nearest door, ignoring the woman beside it, and moved in an awkward trot, waving for him to follow. Once in, she headed in a tizzy for the steaming coffee pot in back. And that's when he spotted the cookies. They were plump chocolate chip with sprinklings of pecans or maybe walnuts, and, because Nehemiah hadn't eaten in days (except for leftover red beans smeared with mustard), he devoured them and, in his frenzy, the crumbs scattered to the floor. Feayo grabbed a bunch, stuffed them in his mouth.

The woman followed them in. But Grandma paid no mind. She carried her cup to the couch, sat down, nodded off. And that's when he had his way, eating an entire plateful, and then, energized by his warmth and fullness, began running about the shop, shrieking, throwing the partially-eaten cookies at Feayo, stumbling, getting up, diving on top of Feayo. Feayo was throwing punches, giggling, running about; Nehemiah had to chase and tackle him, giddy, zapped with happiness.

"Shut the fuck up and sit your ass down!" Grandma Zella bellowed, her tone grave with authority. She was sitting up, wide-eyed.

But he was having too much fun. He cuffed Feayo with the back of his hand. Feayo tackled him, pulled him down.

"Nehemiah," Grandma scolded, "why the hell you smack your cousin? Feayo, you behave your ass ... Feayo, get off Nehemiah. You boys, you gotta mind. I'm warning you, be good! I ain't gone take no shit this time."

Nehemiah felt his Grandma's hand. She was jerking him to the couch. She grabbed Feayo by the ear, her eyes like daggers. She sat at the far left corner of the couch, daring them to misbehave. But Nehemiah couldn't control himself. For the first time in his life he felt warm and full and gratified, a relief so overwhelming it released a craziness in him that found him grabbing irises from a vase and stuffing them in Feayo's mouth. He stood on the couch, his muddy shoes leaving tracks on the crushed blue velvet, and leaped across the table to make his getaway. But he didn't quite make the leap, one foot catching the edge of the table, capsizing it, the vase shattering.

"Now wait a fucking minute," Grandma exploded. She tried getting up but it was much too hard a task so she shook her fist instead. "Nehemiah, why you act this way? Pick up them flowers and that poor woman's vase."

"Stay right where you are!"

It was the woman who'd followed them in. Nehemiah waited for her next words. She yanked off her gloves — "Don't touch *anything!*" — and scrambled to pick up the vase, stooping and cradling the larger pieces. Nehemiah could feel her fury as she made her way to the desk and dropped them in a can. She returned, picked up the remaining shards. "I just want you to leave," she said.

Lines fanned out across Grandma's face. She looked older, frailer, than her seventy-eight years. Feayo didn't move. He gazed mournfully at the woman then at the muddy prints on the couch. Nehemiah waited to feel some shame for the embarrassment he caused but the more he thought about what happened the more hilarious it became and so he waited for the next stage in this ridiculous turn of events. Grandma tried rising. Feayo got up and helped her.

"My name's Zella ..." She approached the woman. "Zella Thyra Theophile. I'm so pleased to meet you, darlin'." She stood awkwardly, extending her hand. The woman turned away.

Grandma patted her shoulder. "I'm so sorry ..." A sadness clouded her face. "You know, I try to teach 'em manners but it ain't quite working out."

The woman caught her sorrow but couldn't quite overcome her fury. Grandma took in her anger, seeming to be struggling to say more, something important, it seemed to Nehemiah. The woman turned her eyes to the couch before heading to the back room. That's when Grandma called out, her strong, hopeful voice breaking the awful silence. "I'm gonna take care of this," she boomed. "You hear me, darlin'? Going right to my place now and get me some Woolite. This sofa gone look brand new aft' I get done with it. I'm gone dab a little on a wet cloth and it's gone take it right out. And honey ..." Grandma brightened, putting energy behind her words, "I can't tell you how sorry I am 'bout that vase. That fool Nehemiah, he gone buy you 'nother soon as he get some cash."

Grandma made her way to the door but stopped when she heard the woman: "You don't have to do that. I just want you to leave," she said. "You take your boys with you."

A disturbance swept through Grandma. She stood frozen in her spot, looking like she wanted to give it another try, utter new words of hope, use that thundering voice of hers, but still another change came over her and, with a shudder, gave up all pretense and simply became herself. "Honey," she said softly. "Honey ... I'm begging you, *please* don't put us out ..."

Urgency. Nehemiah felt it. He couldn't move, hanging on her every word. But Grandma remained silent, hands cradling her face, and then she bent to pick up the irises. It took enormous effort; once or twice she'd lose her balance but always righted herself. Feayo, that deep melancholy never leaving his eyes, as if he were chronically used to chaos, stood up and put the table right. Nehemiah did his part, picking up crumbs, retrieving irises.

The woman came to Grandma, took the flowers from her hand, and asked her to sit down. Grandma shook her head. "No, honey, I gotta get going. Gotta get me something and clean that couch of yours."

"It's not necessary," the woman insisted. "I have Woolite in back. You look worried. What's wrong?"

"*We ain't got no heat.*" She was looking straight at the woman as if she just might be her savior before shrugging, bowing her head. Seeing a pool of water from the broken vase, Grandma searched for something and, not finding it, hurried to the back room. She returned with paper towels, got down on her knees, began wiping.

There was something in the woman's eyes. Pity. Nehemiah felt it.

"You say you have no heat?"

"Them boys gone get *pneumonia*." Grandma stopped wiping. "And I ain't got the money pay no hospital bill."

"Why don't you have heat?"

"No electricity. They turn it off. I can't pay the bill. It was huge. Now my pipes done froze. There's no light and it's like zero degrees inside. If we can jus stay the night, honey, the cold gone be gone. It don't last forever. *Please,* we'll do anything." She seemed about to cry, her voice thick with worry. "We'll mop, dust, sweep ... Then we'll be gone — you won't ever see us again."

"You mean sleep on the floor?"

"We'll get blankets. Jus for the night. *Please* ... Maybe tomorrow night if the cold still linger. It'll be warm after that and my boys they'll be in school and we'll be outta your hair, I promise. We won't be back — I cross my heart!"

"Do you have friends?" the woman wanted to know.

Grandma looked at her. She seemed to be thinking something deep, sizing up the woman, something Nehemiah couldn't understand, but without judgment or anger. She motioned for Feayo to help her up and he did, and she went to the back and returned without the dirty towels. Grandma stood tall and dignified, staring without expression, and then, without taking her eyes off the woman, though Nehemiah knew it was meant for him, said, "Okay, let's get going." She waddled to the door, Nehemiah and Feayo following after her. And as they got to the door, the woman called out, "Wait ...

"... I didn't mean you can't stay. I was just wondering why you can't stay with friends. Or maybe in a shelter. The Baptist Mission ... Bridge House ... They take in the homeless on nights like this. But I didn't say you couldn't. If you have no other place to go, I can't let you sleep on the freezing ground."

"If they so much as *breathe* wrong," Grandma shuddered, shaking her fist to make the point, "I'll crack their fucking heads. We won't be no bother. I know you won't be sorry."

"My name's Annie." She came over. "Annie Ajami. You get your blankets and pillows. For now, we'll store them in the back room. Tonight, you can sleep on the couch and the boys on the floor. I sleep here, too — the cot in back. You see, I make my home here — temporarily, to cut costs. But I haven't told the landlord. It's only for a short time. There's a tiny bathroom with a shower so you and the boys can wash up. But you can't stay after Sunday night. You'll have to make other accommodations."

"Honey, you the answer to my *prayers*," Grandma said, dramatically. She grabbed her hand and shook it. "I been praying to Father Seelos."

"Father who?"

"Francis Xavier Seelos, the Redemptorist priest 'round the corner. Or he was till he pass on."

"When was that?"

"'67."

"1967?"

"No, honey. 1867. He was 48 when he pass, jus one year after coming to N'awlins to be pastor of St. Mary's Assumption Church. He was young, die from the yellow fever. But the man gone be a saint. They done beatified him in St. Peter's Square couple years ago. All they needs is proof of one more miracle."

Nehemiah once again took Grandma's hand and, with Feayo trailing behind, made sure she wouldn't fall as they made their way to the sidewalk before turning the corner to get their things.

*

Annie watched as they walked out. The younger boy couldn't be more than nine. He had bright, effulgent eyes and dark, bushy hair. The older, maybe fourteen, surely no more than that. He seemed to follow the lead of the younger, showing less confidence, it seemed to Annie. She looked about for what to give them to keep them occupied. Boxes of books in the back room still needed to be unpacked. Price stickers had to be put on some of the used books. She hadn't finished putting supplies away, the pens, scotch tape, the special order forms and wrong shipment forms, the stationery and envelopes. This, they could do. A day. Two. And then they would be gone.

She made a mental note to put the pistol away. Young boys and handguns were an explosive combination, and she would take it out of the drawer and hide it somewhere, maybe under the cot. But as she headed to the door to watch them disappear, she forgot about the Colt .45, thinking more about the icy cold that seemed to be turning even grimmer. That morning, she'd read in *The*

16

Times-Picayune, a snowstorm was wreaking havoc across a dozen states, causing electricity to go out, flights to be grounded, dumping snow in double digits on the East Coast. She was lucky living in the Big Easy, where there was practically no such thing as snow-sleet-ice. But still, it felt unbearable. She never quite got used to cold, having been raised in the gentle clime of the Mississippi Gulf Coast, in a home across from the beachfront highway, some 75 miles east of here. She shivered, was about to close the door, when out of the corner of her eye she saw a man.

He was headed her way: gaunt, about six-foot-four, bedraggled, unkempt. His clothes, threadbare. He wore brown corduroy pants showing stains and dirt, a frayed white shirt, brown corduroy jacket, and ankle-high boots. He sported a dark mustache. His beard was streaked with silver. His hair was dark but with the same striking silvery streaks and, though he wore wire-rimmed glasses, she could see his eyes were blue. He didn't look very old, despite the silvery hair. Something told her he couldn't be much older than in his mid-to late thirties.

But there was something world-weary about him, and the look of him moved her. He seemed cosmopolitan, almost cerebral. Intelligence shone in his eyes. He was looking at her and then at the overhanging sign, *Faulkner & Friends,* and as she waited for him inside, she knew instinctively his intent. She didn't know the man at all but recognized the facial expression. He was a hunter — searcher — and she was positive he would come in. And, sure enough, he stepped inside, made his way to the fiction shelves, his careful, penetrating eyes perusing the titles. He was looking for a certain book. She knew it. She came over, asked if she could help.

My first customer.

*

Marvin Everillo considered the woman's offer but turned his attention back to the shelves of books. After all, he was the independent sort, self-reliant, at least he tried to be. And as he wandered through the stacks, he was disappointed the book wasn't there. He wanted it. Really wanted it. He needed to read it one more time, needed to know if it had found a home in this little shop in the 2100 block of Magazine, and so he condescended to turn her way.

She stepped forward: "Is there something I can *find* for you?"

"I'm looking for a novel," he said. "It's called *Second-Story Window.*"

"Oh my God." She gave a little cry. "It's my favorite! It's by Marvin Everillo. Wasn't he the most talented man? It's over here." She led him to a bookcase that had been marked, 'New Orleans Writers.'

He thought he would tease her, have a little fun, there was no harm in that, and so he asked what it was about, and she went on for twenty minutes, and he wasn't expecting that.

She told him it was about a man who discovers that the love of his life is schizophrenic. The woman disappears and the man learns she is living in a down-at-the-heels rooming house on Laurel Street in Uptown New Orleans and, one morning before dawn, he goes and waits for her in his car, sits and waits outside the rooming house and watches, sees an old nun entering a church across the street, sees banana trees in the front yard of the church, their green fruit clustered near the top. And then he turns back to the rooming house and sees a pale glow of light illuminating rose curtains in a second-story window, and he knows she is there. He gets out of his car and yells to her, yells at the illumination, a sign of her real intelligence.

The woman gushed on and on about the lyricism of the writing, the vivid, breathtaking prose, the perceptions and insights of the protagonist, the imagery that made her feel as if she were physically present, the theme that went beyond mere love story to an understanding of life itself, and that it had won a Pulitzer Prize for Fiction the year it had been published less than a decade earlier.

But she wasn't quite finished. She went on to tell him that the book was beautiful in the way James Agee's *Let Us Now Praise Famous Men* was beautiful, in its camera-eye inspection of every detail of things and men, "the wrecked quilt nearly dead-gray with dirt," the babies Katy and Flora Merry Lee who lived in the sharecroppers' shack where Agee stayed to write his documentary masterpiece, transforming them from mere objects and entities to precious creations of God, exultant and relevant and brilliant in their own right. She said the mind of Marvin Everillo was very much like that of James Agee. But that Marvin Everillo had disappeared a long time ago and nobody knew where he went. Certainly, nothing of his had ever been published again, the man and his talent vanquished forever. She said she was grateful someone else appreciated his work as much as she did.

She removed the book and gave it to him.

"Here," she said.

"May I sit down?"

"Be my guest."

He approached the armchair and settled in it, cradling the book in both his hands. Before he opened it, he brushed a finger lovingly across its cover. It was a hardback, a first edition. He felt pleasure in touching it, a part of himself that gave him pride. Then he had the urge to tell her exactly who he was.

"You know," he began, "he didn't actually win it. He was only a finalist for the Pulitzer."

"In my opinion," she replied, "he *should* have won it. It's as close to a masterpiece as I've ever read."

"That's very nice of you to say."

"Why nice?"

"Because I'm the one who wrote it. But you can't tell anybody that."

"Oh my God." She stepped back.

"You promise you won't tell? That person doesn't exist anymore. I go by the name Leo now."

She seemed to fumble all over herself to ask a dozen questions and that was when an old lady and two young boys stepped in. The old lady chattered noisily, carrying a bottle of fabric wash and paper towels, the boys hauling blankets and pillows. The old woman instructed the boys to take them to the back and then plopped down on the couch. "Oh Lord," she said, sighing. She dabbed liquid on a section of towel and delicately wiped the spots.

Marvin eyed the old woman, a bit unnerved by the distraction, but soon began seeing her in a different light, a journalist's observation of a human subject, scrutinizing everything: her movements, the resonance of her voice, the boys' reactions as they fluttered about.

The old woman commanded the boys to ask if there was anything they could do to help, and soon they were given chores in the back and that's when Marvin went back to his book, ignoring the old woman as she sat in the corner of the couch, appearing comfortable, warm against the inclement weather, lost in her pleasant reveries.

*

So this is what I've become. I'm a bookseller now.

Annie was amazed as she gazed about, her attention focused on the shelves of books. A thrill ran through her looking at her precious, magnificent books and then her mind wandered back to her former life. Memories of the past came flooding back, a shame overwhelming her as she recalled the night of terror. And in that moment of recollection, she forgot where she was, her new life, the shop, and that familiar compulsion returned, the longing to be six feet under where no one could see or hear her, where she'd be concealed by a stained-wood coffin that shielded her from life itself. How fervently she wished she'd never been born so that the loss she was responsible for, never could have happened. Wouldn't that be marvelous?

The world better off, her husband. It'd broken her heart what she'd done; but nothing could take that back. And so she was left to create her own destruction without bothering anyone else.

Faulkner & Friends.

Built upon a fallacy. Her own kind. She looked around the room. It was past noon, no customers. All her research — the books, studies — had been right. The mom and pop stores, indies, they called them, were dropping like military targets, now only 15 percent of the market. And those booksellers still surviving were taking home as compensation less than $6,000 a year, those with small shops like hers; she'd read it in a financial survey the American Booksellers Association put out.

And still, knowing that, she'd persisted in her efforts. It was either that or kill herself. She'd sold the house where she and her husband lived, bought the books, and signed the lease. She knew she'd probably never sell enough books to recoup her investment. And the insanity of it all was that while she suspected the business would not survive, she went ahead with it anyway. It was truly the only thing in life that meant anything at all to her.

Two o'clock, no customers. *Stop being such a goddamn pessimist.* She watched Everillo read. He'd never moved, never bothered to take lunch. He was nearly three-quarters of the way finished, a fast reader, but no surprise. And as though a compulsion had taken over, for she could no longer endure her pathetic thoughts, she went over and stood before him. "Excuse me," she blurted out, "you're a learned man. I would be honored if you'd lead a discussion group."

His legs were crossed at the ankles, his hand touching the page, his amusement showing.

"What is it about me that looks learned?" he asked.

She paused to consider that.

Zella did not seem impressed. "If I could wash your pants and jacket," she sniffed, "you'd not only look learned, you'd look *clean*, young man."

His eyes shifted from her to Annie.

"I mean," Annie continued, "I need somebody to be the facilitator for a book discussion club I plan to start. Will you do me the honor?"

He smiled.

"What makes you think I have the qualifications?"

"Nobody," she whispered fiercely, "has better qualifications than *you*. *Nobody*. But if you'd rather not …" Her voice faded. She made her way to the front and sat behind the desk. She bent her forehead over her folded hands. "It's just one more stupid thing …" Wearily, she looked up, gazed out of the display window to see people passing on the sidewalk: a bent, old woman with a black gap between her teeth; a man walking several paces behind, dressed like a hobo, wild eyed, muttering. She had the sudden urge to go and inspect her new surroundings.

She'd leased this space with all the optimism in the world. She'd *wanted* to set up shop in this poor section of Magazine. She'd *wanted* to do good, help the poor, the young, the elderly to discover the world of books. She had so many plans. But she'd become frightened as time went by that she may have made a mistake. It takes money to own a bookshop — all the great accomplishments and noble intentions could not substitute for money — and all the experts had warned, "Location is everything," if you wanted to make a profit in this business. She decided to take a walk around the block, get acquainted with her new neighbors.

She announced to her startled guests she was leaving and ordered them out of the shop. She'd be back in fifteen minutes. They could come back later. She shooed them out and, without bothering to put on a coat, locked the shop and headed in the direction she'd seen Zella come from, turning the corner on St. Andrew Street, toward the Mississippi River. Around the corner, there were only two blocks before everything dead-ended. As she walked along the first block, she passed a building with a sign, *St. Thomas Health Service*. At the end of the block across the street stood a row of houses: dilapidated clapboards with peeling paint in greens and pinks and blues, two of them dingy camelbacks with collapsing porches and leaning columns. A decrepit white sofa turned gray from age, adorned one porch. Three grocery carts littered the concrete yard. A house hovering behind a pile of yard trash displayed a message painted on a board sealing a window: *Don't shit in toilet back up floor.*

Farther on, several doors down, stood the last house on the block: a clapboard with a pitched shingled roof overrun with vines, the windows and doors boarded up, a sign nailed to the facade: *No Trespassing. Keep Out.*

Beyond this stretched acres of fallow land with great mounds of dirt piled here and there and a dirt strip in the center, in working progress to become a road. Beer bellied men in dark blue shirts and hard hats sat on machines, looking down on men digging in pits. She turned around, headed toward a cross street named Constance, parallel to and behind Magazine. And there on both sides of Constance were large brown brick buildings. They were a hundred and fifty years old, she guessed, with broad windows framed in dark green and religious statuettes in yards.

On the right side of Constance was St. Alphonsus Art & Cultural Center; on the left, plaques baring the legends: St. Alphonsus Parish & Rectory; Father Seelos Museum; Redemptorist Elderly Apartments; and St. Mary's Assumption Catholic Church.

The church, a German baroque revival structure, appeared as tall as a seven-story building, its stained-glass windows at least 25-feet high, its steeple green and gold. Like everything else, the church was brown brick, intricately crafted, with niches, arches and crosses. It was enclosed behind a 12-foot tall brick and wrought-iron gate. She tried entering the church where it fronted on a side street, but its massive mahogany doors were bolted.

She turned right on the side street — Josephine — heading toward Magazine and realized that almost everyone she'd encountered was black: black men at a corner idling in chairs tilted against a wall, drinking from bottles in brown paper bags, others sitting on stoops or meandering down the sidewalk.

One man at the corner: "Even if they sold it for a *dollar* —" he barked, sitting on the sidewalk, leaning against a masonry wall.

"— They'd get 100% profit," interrupted his pal.

"— They'd *still* get 100% profit," the man repeated excitedly, "cuz they got it for *nothin'*."

The few whites she encountered looked equally hard up: a woman with a round face and tumorous belly donning a shirt and jeans, hair parted in the center and tied at the nape of her neck; a gaunt man in baggy Bermudas oblivious to the cold, tattoos covering his calf, an angry rash his neck.

Welfare city, she thought. *Nothing but bums and derelicts.*

Doesn't anyone dress for the weather? But who was she to talk, she without her coat, shivering in the arctic freeze? *We all must want to commit suicide.*

She headed back to the shop.

On her way back she shivered, this time from regret, realizing her fatal error. She'd once entertained the notion of opening in a different part of Magazine, in the affluent Uptown section. One day she'd taken a stroll with that in mind. It'd been a chilly November morning. The sounds of the street echoed in the air: the humming of car engines, roaring of big trucks. She'd heard the sharp thick bark of a dog, the long, delicate shrill of a bird. She'd passed Cajun Boy's Seafood, with its logo on the window: a crawfish surrounded by the words, *Pinch the tail, suck the head.*

She'd passed antique shops and shoe repair shops and Persian rug shops and peered through display windows to see sculptures, statuettes, pottery, porcelain vases. She remembered seeing brilliant red and orange Hawaiian ginger shooting out of containers from behind a florist's window and, on its front lawn, baskets of cotton bolls. She'd entered a brass bed store, it's down comforters on expensive beds, and Carol Robinson's Gallery, displaying silver and gold sculptures titled Chopin and Bach, and, after leaving both establishments, she decided, *Here is where I'll open shop.* And then she immediately dismissed that idea because she couldn't afford the high rent.

Besides, she could do so much more good in a less affluent area. She would mentor poor kids, bring them to the shop, tutor them in reading, let them take home a book. Hold writing contests for inmates or let old folks write reviews for her newsletter. She couldn't afford a better area and that might be a blessing.

Now, reality had set in.

She rounded the corner to her shop.

They were huddled against the door: Zella, the boys, Leo — shivering. She unlocked the door, letting everybody in, and, when they had settled in their favorite spots, Leo in the armchair, the boys on the couch, Zella, as if continuing with a conversation long ago started, turned to Leo.

"You know who my best friend is? The city," Zella told him. "N'awlins's my best friend. And once a year," she said happily, "we spend the day together. I drop what I'm doing and go out and enjoy myself. I do my favorite thing: take the streetcar to Café Du Monde and have *café au lait*. I sit out on a bench in Jackson Square, hear the chiming of cathedral bells, the whining of the organ grinder. I sit in the shade of a mulberry tree and listen to a lotta gossip.

"Once, these gals from Covington was talking, 'bout how the shrink-hubby of the artist one gal rents her cottage from done kill hisself and how her friend's sister die in a car wreck after getting out the nuthouse, and how the dance partner of the other gal gets whacked by his sissy lover, how a monk from the Benedictine monastery marries a local nun and how that nun's other boyfriend's so goddamn pissed he gets a gun and shoots hisself. That town's one crazy fucker. Now jus 'bout now I'm getting hungry. So I get myself a muffuletta then go to Harrah's to play the slots. Then I get my fat ass back on the streetcar and start heading home."

Zella smiled blissfully, reliving her good memories.

Leo nodded, half amused.

"Hey, Zella," Annie called out, "what's going on with all that digging?"

It was three o'clock, no customers.

"Building a road. They gone connect the new road with St. Andrew," Zella told her, "and it gone go all the way through the complex."

"What complex?"

"Didn't you know? There gone be apartments back there and a shopping mall. Done tore down the St. Thomas housing project to do it. And in the middle of the complex gone be a Wal-Mart Superstore."

Annie gasped.

"And they gone have a big book section with discount prices." Zella lowered her voice. "Better look out."

Annie sat down.

"You didn't know?" Zella swung around. "Ain't been reading the paper?"

It was amazing to Annie she hadn't heard. In the old days, she'd never let anything get past her. Off and on in the years she'd planned her shop, she'd done all kinds of research to prepare and keep informed. She'd joined the ABA; sought advice from the Small Business Administration; interviewed nearly every bookseller in town to see how business was progressing; met with the director of the Small Business Development Center, who was so impressed by her business plan he'd asked if he could teach it to his students; met with a lawyer to form a Limited Liability Company; met with a publisher's rep to pre-order her stock; even flew to a seminar in Chicago to learn how to operate a bookshop.

But everything conspired to discourage her: the giant discount Barnes & Noble announced plans to locate in the city; the ABA financial survey revealed that the average profits for member stores measured one cent out of every sales dollar. Grudgingly, she abandoned her plan.

It took the darkest day of her life to make her change her mind. In America, she believed, all sorts of opportunities were possible. But it was hard to have the spirit and courage to follow through. She'd long ago lost faith. And then one Sunday morning, on her way to Catholic Mass, she heard a woman's voice on the radio: "What do you need reminding of?" The voice was talking to her. "That those dreams in your heart, they weren't put there to torment you. They were put there because God knew that you could do it."

A dream was something you conceived for your life and believed in enough to follow.

And so here she was.

"It looks like they're just beginning," Annie mumbled, trying to reassure herself. She stood up, faced the door. "It'll take at least a year before the Wal-Mart's finished. Why, they've barely plowed the ground. And by then I'll have steady customers. I will *not* give up." She turned to Marvin (she must remember to call him Leo), now walking over to a shelf and putting away a book. He picked up another.

"What do you say?" she said to him. "Will you be my facilitator?"

She could hear the panic in her voice.

"What exactly do you want me to do?"

"Lead the discussion. Pick a book that interests you. I'll put a notice in the paper. I'll announce the title and date and that we'll have free food and wine." She strained to sound natural.

"Just put a sign in the window," he said. "You don't need to go to all that trouble."

"I don't think we'll attract many readers around here. I've seen the neighborhood," she said. "I've got to attract people from Uptown and the Garden District — people who *read*. I've got to find people with *money*." Her eyes bore into his. Seeing something in them that comforted her, she reached out her hand to him. "I forgot to tell you, my name's Annie. And you said I'm to call you Leo?"

"That's right, I go by Leo." He took her hand. "I don't know why you can't get somebody else. It's not the kind of thing I do."

"I have nobody else."

"Well then," he said, "you've got me for this one time."

"I know you're smart. I know you're brilliant. I'm the luckiest girl in the world to run into you. So who are your favorite writers?"

"The Russians. Tolstoy, Dostoevsky."

"And your favorite book?"

"War and Peace."

"Why?"

"It's the greatest book ever written."

"It's over fourteen hundred pages." She frowned. "That may be a little long."

"For what?"

"Our group. Let's pick something ... not quite as intimidating."

"How about Dostoevsky, *The Brothers Karamazov.*"

"Maybe not. I'm sorry, but we'll attract more people if we pick something more ... contemporary. What author do you like who's living?"

"I don't like anybody living."

"I'll tell you what ..." Annie went to the coffee maker, poured a half cup. "We'll do it this way." She poured another and handed it to him. "Besides Dostevoesky and Tolstoy, who else are your favorite writers?"

"Faulkner, Joyce, Huxley, Dos Passos, Henry James, Naipaul ..."

"That's it," she said excitedly. She brought him cream and sugar. "Let's go with Faulkner. He's perfect — and fitting, since he's the namesake for my shop. Pick one of his books, I'll prepare a notice."

"*Light in August,*" he mused. "By far, his best." His hand shook as he poured the cream. "Better than *The Sound And The Fury.* A hundred times better than *Sanctuary.*" He brought the coffee to his lips and it nearly spilled over the rim from the trembling of his hand. He placed the cup on a side table, opened the new book. She hadn't noticed the tremor before. Perhaps it had been there when she'd handed him *Second-Story Window* and she hadn't seen it. Sometimes she didn't pay attention when she was preoccupied or distracted. Now, she was curious as to its cause. But her thoughts shifted to the coming event and she felt an overwhelming relief.

She touched his hand and it stopped trembling.

II. bum in the hot seat

Marvin Everillo woke with a heavy weight inside his head, his nose and fingers numb, and as he struggled to get to his feet, he felt as if he might pass out, a lightness, dizziness, almost overpowering him. He coughed — a hacking cough — and as he lay there for a few moments more to gather strength, he heard the loud voices of a couple passing him on the sidewalk, animated, ignoring him, their voices collapsing into murmurs as they casually drifted off. He opened one eye, measuring the day's brightness to estimate the time. Judging by his usual getting up habits and the brilliance of the sun, he figured it was perhaps a little past noon. He could feel the cutting winds, and his fingers, nearly frozen, caused him more concern than the pain inside his head. *I must get up*, he thought, *I need a drink*. He remembered he had no money and the bottles of the night before were empty. He forced himself to his feet: there was a task awaiting him.

He knew what day it was; he never forgot such things.

He rubbed his hands together and stepped away from the thin blanket. He was in an alley between two buildings, in a space no bigger than six by four, a space so small his feet stuck out onto the sidewalk when he slept. The night light from the art gallery to the right of him pointed down on him and to his left a house, a shotgun double, was painted bright yellow with a red door. Two black garbage bags filled with his belongings lay within inches of where he'd placed his head. And parked in front of him on the street was an old car with rusted hood and seat cushions ripped apart, exposing their stuffings. Leaning heavily against the brick side of the gallery, shuffling forward until the bricks ended, he forced himself onto the sidewalk, moving in slow, mechanical strides, head bowed, looking like a wound-down robot. He made his way to

Magazine Street where he would use the john at Friendly's Bar and splash water on his face then head for the shop, where there would be wine to drink before the task began, calming him, giving him courage, helping him get through it, helping him talk to strangers about Joe Christmas and Lena Grove and the middle-aged spinster whose partly severed head had turned clean around.

He had an obligation, perhaps his last, certainly not his first, and he believed in discharging obligations though his actions in the past decade certainly made a lie of that. But then that was in the past when he was broken and ill, and he was better than that now.

And he believed people were capable of change and should be given second chances. He was giving himself a second chance. If not, why bother to get up in the morning? And he would do his best, with all the resolve left in him.

*

Emma Rose Brewer sat in the second row, near enough to the moderator's chair where she could see and hear everything. Dressed in her black and orange animal print cardigan, her matching long-sleeved shell and black pull-on pants, Emma Rose was a bit early, the first to arrive as was her custom, and her plump thigh, lifted in an ambitious attempt to transcend the other but failing, returned to its original position as a paper plate filled with appetizers rested in her lap.

She popped a sausage bread square into her mouth and saw the man arrive. Her first impression was that he did not belong, someone would have to escort him out, a tramp on the street, the patina of failure as glaring as his seedy pants. It was not the quality of the clothes that stuck out, for he wore a wool shirt jacket, a turtleneck in smoky jade and cotton deck pants in black, but the condition of it that disgusted her, dirty, threadbare, looking as if it'd been slept in.

One could clearly see he was not in tip-top shape by the bloodshot eyes behind the wire-rimmed glasses and the look of exhaustion or illness, and a look that told her he definitely did not want to be here but was here to elude the cold, perhaps. And his face looking drained, the flesh sallow above his silvery beard. It was especially the condition of the clothing, the turtleneck ripped at the waist, the pants perhaps twenty years old, that was repugnant to her, and she shuddered. Taken altogether, the shabby creature shuffling in with his sluggish gate and decrepitude was a disgrace that should be escorted out. Some people have no pride, don't do anything to better their lives, Emma Rose thought as she perused the man while popping a cheese ball in her mouth.

He headed for the table containing the bottles of wine, and nobody stopped him. A woman embraced him, the woman who'd greeted her at the door, her arms enfolding him, pressing her cheek to his, in genuine and joyful welcome, then wrapping an arm around his back as if to hold him up as he lifted a glass and tried pouring the wine, hand shaking, the woman taking the bottle from him and pouring it herself. Someone she knows, Emma Rose surmised. Close friend from the past or dirt poor relative.

The others drifted in for it was now past starting time. Emma Rose recognized a few. Ever since she'd retired six months earlier from her librarian's job at the university, she'd seen several of the individuals now gathered here at past signings and readings and discussions about town: Margie Dawson in her green sweater and bright lipstick and tight pants, her curly red hair pinned up at the back; Ruby Jean Hodorowski in her beige dress and pumps, one of her former colleagues at the library. And there was the art patron Delphine Schlumbrecht and the socialite Megan Hulle and a few others she didn't recognize, an elderly man in faded jeans, trying to be hip with his long white hair tied in back, and an artist-type — appropriately trendy — with a single earring and ponytail.

She saw the derelict glance about the room. He seemed shy, a little afraid, gulping down his wine and pouring himself another. He poured a third one then brought it with him as he took his place in the moderator's chair. *Surely this is a mistake,* Emma Rose thought. *Someone will come get him, force him to surrender his seat, escort him to the back, to one of the chairs facing the moderator's way in the back, far enough away where he's not too close to me.* She was not in the best of moods, whether it was from loneliness or too much time on her hands, she was not sure, but she knew she couldn't tolerate a smelly bum sitting next to her today. Her nerves were shot, as they'd grown increasingly, ever since her supervisor had a talk with her that day six months ago, told her she was making mistakes and forgetting things and maybe she ought to think about early retirement — she'd been forced out to pasture after forty years of devoted work.

It had not been easy forgetting the humiliation of that meeting. It had not been easy trying to bolster her spirits and belief in herself after being told she was half senile and not to be trusted with the tasks she'd performed for more than forty years. And for six months now all there was to do was come to events like this, where her companions were derelicts with bloodshot eyes. And old men frantic to be young. And dilettantes like Megan Hulle with nothing else on their calendars.

She'd tried daily to find a purpose in life, but no one wanted to hire her for even part-time work, a sixty-four-year-old woman. So she kept herself active by scouring the newspaper for lectures and readings and the occasional play, but plays cost money so mostly she ended up at free events. She could at least contribute here; she'd read more books than anyone she knew and could match anyone word for word when it came to intellect. It may be that her short-term memory was shot, but she still possessed a lifetime of knowledge. And the author she knew best was her beloved

William Faulkner, though she was most familiar with
Sanctuary, by far his best work. And the gall of her
supervisor to imply she'd lost her faculties, relegating her to
a life of idleness when she had so much to give the world.
Not like the deadbeat in the moderator's chair *(why hadn't*
someone escorted him out?), not working, not contributing, a
good-for-nothing that fate had put here to spoil another
day.

He sat motionless, languid, only moving once to set
down his glass, and then he looked about nervously until his
eyes locked on hers and, as if he saw in them everything —
her contempt, misgivings, her vile ill will — he cast the
most unhappy look she'd ever seen at the dog-eared
paperback book he clung to.

"My name's Leo," he said softly, signaling for their
attention. "Welcome to the shop. We'll be talking about
Light in August. It's Faulkner's best, in my opinion."

"I don't agree with that."

The voice came from up close. Emma Rose was
shocked to discover the voice was hers, the words shooting
out seemingly without her permission. It didn't bother her
that she disagreed, for she wasn't afraid to be contrary when
the occasion called for it, but she wasn't normally
contentious over trivial things and she'd never in her life
blurted out a comment only to find out afterward it was
hers. It was queer and, most alarming, she heard the ire and
resentment in it.

The bum ignored her. "Who," he went on, "do you
think is the most tragic character?"

"Lena Grove," Ruby Jean shouted after Megan
Hulle whispered in her ear. Emma Rose hated Ruby Jean's
loudness but knew it was due to her being half deaf. It was
the most pathetic combination, Ruby Jean's hearing loss and
her massive craving for attention, for Ruby Jean always liked
to have the first and final word in every conversation; but
she never said anything worthwhile in Emma Rose's

opinion. "Lena Grove!" Ruby Jean repeated, in case nobody heard the first time. "There's nothing more tragic than being abandoned and pregnant."

"She wasn't more tragic than the Rev. Hightower," the artist averred. "He was disgraced because of his wife's affair. He lost his congregation and completely withdrew."

"And he stunk, too," the old man added, delighted to see a smile on a face or two.

"Hightower became the object of rumors," the artist continued earnestly. "He withdrew from society and had no connection with anyone. It was like living a dead man's life."

"But he reentered the world of the living," the bum-moderator said to him. A little color reappeared on his cheeks as he seemed to regain his confidence. He searched the room for faces. "Does anyone know how he did that?"

There was silence. He continued. "He gave Joe Christmas an alibi for his whereabouts the night of the murder. It was his attempt to reenter the world of the living by helping another human being. Some people say that was his redemption."

"He helped a *murderer*," Emma Rose shrieked.

She heard the tone, vehement, hysterical. Where did it come from? It was like some spirit possessing her, playing tricks on her mind, and it would be fascinating if it weren't so disturbing, for the tone of voice was betraying her, a powerful agitation driven by an evil demon exploding from her mouth and she had no control.

A silence followed.

She listened, realizing no one was so much taken aback by what she said as by the frantic tone, shocking her as well, so much so that she squirmed and the paper plate shifted in her lap and a half-eaten spinach pie fell to the floor. She bent to pick it up, lost hold of the plate and it fell as well and Megan Hulle giggled and that infuriated her. Trying to pick up all the food crumbs, her face lifted toward the watching eyes, her own squinting in anger, her mouth shaped in an O as she shrilled, "Joe Christmas was a worthless scumbag murderer."

"You don't have to be so overwrought," Megan stage whispered. Then Megan exploded in giggles, nervous and gleeful. She managed to suppress the giggles and then she said with strained patience: "There are those who see Joe Christmas as a victim of horrible oppression, Emma Rose, because he was part black, which makes him sympathetic, even a Christlike figure."

"But he slit Joanna's *throat,*" said Emma Rose, voice rising. "She cooked his food, gave him a place to sleep, had sex with him, then he goes and slits her throat. Doesn't anybody give a damn?"

The bum-moderator picked up his glass, put it to his lips and emptied it. He shut his eyes as if savoring the wine's comfort, then he looked at her and this time his eyes betrayed no emotion. "Christmas had no identity." It was as if a dead man spoke. His voice was a monotone. "He had no idea who his parents were so he was a cipher to himself and everyone else. That was his tragedy."

"There're lots of folks in this world who don't know who their parents are," she said with contempt. "But that doesn't mean they're supposed to go around killing people." Her hands began to tremble. Her tone took on the injured quality of a wronged child. "Why are you making excuses for him?"

"Certainly I'm not … no one's …" His voice began to falter. He shook his head in disbelief then lowered it and smiled. It was as if he found it amusing she could think he cared enough to give excuses. Slowly, feebly, he set down the glass. When he sat up, he turned to the paperback and leafed through the pages. "There is a scene here where he says …" and he began to read, "… 'I have never broken out of the ring of what I have already done and cannot ever undo ... '" He closed the book but did not lift his eyes from it. "Can't you pity that?"

"No," Emma Rose snapped. "You're making excuses ... making excuses for a *murderer.*"

The bum-moderator looked exhausted. He glanced anxiously at the empty glass, tightened his hold on the paperback, squeezing it and wincing at the same time; and then it seemed as if he were a prisoner chained in lifetime confinement inside some dark and empty hole. Emma Rose couldn't help for a moment pitying him as she suddenly pitied her own life, the failures, the disappointments, all the humiliations, the young boy Russell she took in, who in the end deserted her, the boy who'd run away, and she couldn't bear thinking about her life, thinking about the past, the past that was so hideous. And then the bum-moderator was talking again, this time his voice far away — way off in Alabama or Mississippi, wherever Joe Christmas came from — as he spoke to no one in particular, in words she strained to hear.

"I keep going over the part," he said, "about him thinking it was loneliness he was running from and not himself and the street running on, catlike, and how one place was the same as another to him, but in none of them could he be quiet."

She could tell he had memorized the lines in a book of five hundred pages. He took off his glasses, rubbed his eyes, and she could clearly see the red in them and how he seemed oblivious to everything around him.

He suddenly looked at her intently, and she hadn't expected that. In a disembodied voice, he said, "Have you ever felt like that?"

Emma Rose paused. She said nothing for several moments and all eyes were upon her. His, too, did not waver.

Finally, she said, "Ever felt like what?"

Somebody behind her sighed. The bum showed no expression. He got up, made his way to the wine table. He filled a new glass to the brim and, with his back to all of them, downed it and poured another. She didn't even wait until he finished. She stood up, with his back to her, and shouted: "Look at you — that's your fifth or sixth glass of wine." Then with her hands on hips, said, "Maybe some of us here don't have anything to run away from. And maybe people like you are jealous of people like us. People who don't do anything but work hard all our lives and treat people decently and try to be honest. It's people like you who feel sorry for some cold-blooded, mulatto drifter who just because he's half black and doesn't know who his parents are thinks he can get away with slitting a girl's throat. Look at how you look."

She stretched out an arm and pointed. "Why you don't even have the decency to put on nice clothes. Look at you. Why, one would suspect you've never done a day's work in your life. But no one respects hard work anymore, so you should get along just fine. But don't patronize me because I don't have sympathy for your ne'er-do-well drifter — which is just what *you* are: a ne'er-do-well, deadbeat drifter."

He did not turn. He bent forward toward the table and then his body collapsed, the wine bottles and glasses and hors oeuvres crashing to the floor along with the table. A boy came running toward him from out of nowhere, a black child about nine or ten, yelling, "You leave him alone..." and then, "Leo! Leo!" and grabbing him, holding on, trying to turn him over, then looking at her with hatred in his eyes and yelling, "Shut up!" then at him, "Leo!" The boy glared at her, his black, shimmering eyes heartfelt and frightened, and then he turned back to the bum, his child's arms cradling him and trying to turn him over but the bum was dead weight, perfectly moribund, his skin blanched at the back of the neck and the fingers still clinching the glass as if he couldn't bear to let go.

And now an old black woman and an older boy and the white woman who'd welcomed her at the door assembled about the collapsed table and hovered over him, while other members of the gathering, the old man and the artist, stood up; still others — Ruby Jean and Delphine and Megan — remained seated with their mouths agape, eyes fixed on the calamity before them. And now would be a perfect time to leave, Emma Rose thought, another notch in the belt of her own devastation.

III. worst day of my life

Nehemiah thought he heard her calling his name through the thin wall that separated his room from hers. At first, it sounded like a kitten's cries, rising in intensity as he lay upon the mattress under the window that let in the steamy night through the black metal bars. Then he was sure it was no kitten. *"Nehemiah, Nehemiah ..."* — again he heard the cries. He listened, held his breath, but the only sounds came from Casey's Bar down the street, hip-hop and chatter, and a woman's startled shrieks, playful and harmless, rising and falling.

Nehemiah hoped he'd hear no more. And if he did, he would be mistaken; it was a dream or surely a kitten's cries and not what he dreaded come to snatch him from the night and ask more of him than he could ever give, but must. He let out his breath, rubbed his sleepy eyes, lifted himself till he stood barefoot upon the mattress. He glanced through the barred window, seeing next door the partially collapsed wall of a burnt-out Creole cottage through which the ceiling was exposed in a room he'd never entered. The cottage next door on Pauger Street had been torched three times. Once when he'd tried walking through it in his bare feet, his mama stopped him because there were needles on the floor and he knew the scorched building was a heroin den for junkies.

His mama's home away from home — hers and John Elloie — where they spent most of their days. They'd rather be there then where he lingered since his mama took him from Hoffman, where he'd learned reading and math and took naps with his head down, as Tiara Patterson, his teacher, read stories after lunch. His mama had locked him in this shotgun house next to a burnt-out heroin den where she and John Elloie spent their days. Here, on this filthy mattress, he'd lie staring at the window, hearing the eruption of voices echoing from their hideaway.

Why didn't she stay with him? Maybe she was being good by not keeping company, separating him from the scene she never wanted him to see. Why did she take him away from school? He was not the one to say. She had her reasons, though her reasoning had grown cloudy as her body grew thin from the things she did next door, so he could not hold her responsible for decisions he didn't understand. But there was nothing for him to do here, no one to do it with. And he never wanted to go into his mama's room or the kitchen with its sea of trash where there was nothing to eat anyway or the bathroom with its grimy, stopped-up toilet.

There was no hope of escape with the locked doors and barred windows. But he could dream and he could imagine. And sometimes peace settled over his days, easing the terror like a soft summer breeze, and he liked that better than night. This night, he heard the cries, stood rigid before the window. No kitten's cries. And there was no mistaking it: "*Nehemiah ... Nehemiah...*"

He jumped off the mattress, heart pounding, and ran to his mama's room. There, he saw John Elloie with a black-handled steak knife kneeling over her, wearing a look of pure hatred, his right hand raised as it had so many times, only this time holding a knife, and he was plunging the blade inside her. "*... Stop ...*" John Elloie turned. "*Get away from my mama ...*" He reached for the knife, the other hand pressing against John Elloie, as the still and silent figure lay trapped beneath the man, unable ever again to break a young boy's heart.

He woke up at Charity. It was a month before they took the bandages off. Then everything was the way it had been before she took him away from Hoffman. He was back again in class, back with Grandma Zella, where he'd lived most of his days before his mama got to missing him. He was with Feayo again, back where he was before his mama changed her mind about giving him up to Grandma, then withdrawing him from Hoffman, refusing even to let Grandma visit him or his own daddy, not that his daddy gave a damn, claiming he didn't know where to find his son, though Pauger Street was less than a mile from where his daddy lived.

And after she died — stabbed 49 times, the knife in John Elloie's hand lodged inside her head, lifting her from the bed, as he tried to strike again — everyone said bad things about her. Never about John Elloie, who was crazy, after all, born of a mama who used a hatchet to behead her own stepdaddy then later hanged herself. John Elloie was a junkie, John Elloie, insane. So he wasn't to blame. But they blamed everyone else. They didn't think he heard them whispering at the funeral, blaming everyone for what happened: the district attorney's office who didn't punish his mama after someone reported how she spent her days; the Office of Community Services, which closed its own neglect case and washed its hands of Nehemiah; his daddy who swore he didn't know how his own son lived or where, but he knew — how could he not? — even his teacher, Tiara Patterson, who once visited the shotgun house when he was still enrolled at Hoffman and saw the trail of trash and did nothing; the neighbors who knew he was locked up, blaming everyone for their part in the destruction of a child (everyone except John Elloie), but most of all blaming her.

He would never blame her. Even the worst days in his room were better than living without her — the beautiful, worrying eyes, the tender touch of her. No one knew the loss of love better than her. And every time she held him the pain within him ceased, replaced by an overwhelming joy. He would not let anyone talk bad of her. His only comfort after her death, the memories of the time he spent with her, his body sheltering her from blows, hands wiping away the tears and washing away the blood, bandaging and holding her as she cried, his comfort now the comfort he gave, brought back to him in the solitude of his grieving memories.

*

Marvin remembered the mute faces. He'd never forget. Not the wooden table where he'd sat, or his girl, Lola, standing behind him or the books stacked on the table, books that contained his words, or the sixty or so anonymous faces, their bodies settled in folding chairs or standing amid shelves, anticipatory and breathless, staring as he stared back. The bookstore had opened three weeks earlier, started by a judge he knew from the federal courts in a run-down part of Camp Street less than a mile from his own apartment on Coliseum Square, across from the park. He would never forget the sandwiches on trays, the guest book by the door, reminders of a different style of life, arousing in him a strange nostalgia. Or the middle-aged man with dark, wavy hair and an air of suppressed exhilaration who came forth from the sea of faces and asked that Marvin sign the book he'd bought. And on the title page the man had written his name and prison number — 61737-053 — so proud was he of the past they both shared — and all Marvin had to do was scribble a few words and then his name.

He remembered the tableau, remembered Lola with her strawberry-blonde hair cascading down her shoulders and his astonishment at the strangers' admiration or that they deemed him worthy of their time when not that very long ago he'd idled away his own lying on a prison cot. The silence was different in that prison cell in Texas, where no eyes gazed upon him, the monotony like insecticide settling in a fine mist, the solitude unbearable, forcing him to a place he normally would never go.

Something miraculous and mystical had been hiding in the corner of that cell he shared with no one. It reminded him of his childhood days when he'd ascend the attic stairs of the turn-of-the-century Colonial home where he and his parents lived, to explore the relics and family heirlooms. This time, though, the climbing had been arduous, the exploration itself a grueling search in the dark and heat, the discovery bringing forth incalculable grief and suffering. It brought him face to face with the artifacts of his youth, the yearbook with its long-lost messages from friends who'd loved him once. It'd been a long time since someone loved him. And he'd forgotten them, forgotten love.

This thing hiding in the cell was miraculous, delicate as a child's longing, sacred as a baptismal blessing, exquisite as the ghost voices rising above words scribbled on the pages of the yearbook long ago, causing grief in memory of what love was once. And it was that mysterious thing that led him to the attic, where his brain was wrapped in rhythm and language and technique he never knew he had. It had shadowed him as he explored and discovered and retrieved and made sense of, stood by him to give courage and patience and understanding during seven long years in the dark creating something out of nothing.

Seven years had been his punishment for robbing three banks, reaping enough reward from the misadventure to spend a few weekends in Vegas, a few nights with working girls, a few rounds at the poker table, till the cops came to get him. Marvin wasn't hard to find. He'd never used a gun, though they couldn't have known that at the time (he'd been clever in his deceit). In prison he'd written the bank teller to apologize, though in his introspective moments he deemed the letter itself an unkindness, heaping more fear upon the girl, though he hadn't meant to do that.

He'd only intended to kill himself, suicide-by-cop. He'd tried to do it in other ways. Once, after his wife left him, he closed the windows of his apartment and turned on the gas oven and drank himself to sleep but, to his astonishment, woke up the next morning as alive as ever. Once, he drove his car off a wharf but survived that excursion as he'd survived drinking bouts, mental wards, drunk tanks, jail. In that cell in federal prison, there had been no hiding place and only one place to escape to.

Marvin would never forget: the eyes staring as if he were a Harry Winston diamond. The talent was in the genes, the critics wrote. His father had been a senior editor for a New York publishing house. The technique, of course, (they said) came from his prestigious education: the American School in Switzerland, then college at Cornell. But he knew what the critics celebrated came from that trip to the attic, where something had taken him. He'd won a writing prize in prison and nearly won the Pulitzer. He thought his life would change with the acclaim and money but nothing changed, not the drinking, not the remorse for the countless spineless acts it was too late to rectify. (How could he forget the girlfriend whose face was partially paralyzed after a reckless ride with him on a Harley?) And as the promise vanished, so did the money.

He vowed never to drink again after they let him out of prison. And for a while he kept his vow. It was after he'd found that place on Coliseum Square and begun a second novel that he'd started back. The novel was a disappointment; he'd hauled it to the park one night and dumped it in a trash bin on his way to Katz & Bestoff Drug Store to pick up a fifth of vodka, and, after that, couldn't control it, the drinking then the drugging, during the many late-night parties that made it all but impossible to ascend to that place where the treasures were.

Someone told him once that whenever one goes through hell to just keep on walking through it. And he would follow that advice. Maybe he couldn't stop drinking but he wasn't the man he was before, plotting his demise, disbelieving in miracles. The one thing he knew today was that he *wanted* to live, if for no other reason than to discover where the thing went that had shadowed him in the attic and stood over him as he wrote, palpable and omnipresent as a pencil in his hand, before absconding to foreign places. He had even changed his name — Leo, he'd call himself — so that he could go forth in this world brand new, taking one step at a time, performing each task with grace, till he could find the strength he needed to get back on his feet again.

*

It was noon, seven weeks after the grand opening. Annie still had few customers. The morning had been especially rough: Her landlord had paid a visit.

"Do you think I'm blind?" he asked. "I saw that old woman and her boys sleeping in this room. You don't think I know what's going on?"

"I don't think that, Mr. Zibilich."

"And that bum crashes here too, don't he? I saw him walk in one day and forever be hanging out."

"He doesn't crash here regularly. But he's sick today."

They had been standing in the front room, in front of the cash register.

"And you're crashing here too, ain't you? You're here all hours of the day and night. You don't ever go home. My building *is* your home. You're violating the terms of the lease agreement, now don't you dare deny it!"

"I won't."

"I have a duty to keep up my property. I ain't running no boarding house. If you and your vagrant pals don't stop sleeping here at once, I'll have no choice but to evict you."

Annie said she was sorry. She'd pleaded with him to give her time to find a suitable place to live. She'd wondered why he'd been spying on her and how he'd found the time to see all that? She'd pleaded for her friends as well. The old woman — a grandma with two hungry mouths to feed — had to leave her apartment because she couldn't pay the bills and the man in the back room was very, very ill and down on his luck and needed a place to recuperate.

"I don't give a damn," he told her.

She'd explained she'd wanted them off the property. She couldn't count the number of times she'd almost asked the old woman to leave, but that would mean they'd be out on the street again, her and her boys, and she couldn't have that on her conscience. And that man in the back room never slept here but once, last night, and when he gets better he'll leave — *so help me God, I swear to you!*

"I'm sorry as I can be but I ain't running no charity. And this is how it is: I'll give you a month and a half, till April 1st, that's fair, to find other sleeping accommodations," he said, "or you'll have to take your business elsewhere."

"I don't mean any disrespect, Mr. Zibilich, but I don't understand why it's not allowed. There's a sink and shower and stove in back."

"Because the previous tenant who lived in the back room caused big trouble and I forbid it after that."

"What kind of trouble?"

"A rape took place in that back room," Mr. Zibilich, an old man, blushed. "He brought a woman back there after a night of heavy boozing."

"Did you evict him?"

He rolled his eyes. "Didn't have to. A jury did. He's spending fifteen years in prison."

"Oh," she gasped. "What kind of business was he in?"

"Now, listen!" He shook his finger. "You're trying to change the subject. You knew perfectly well crashing on these premises was off limits *before* you rented the space. It's spelled out bold and clear in the lease agreement. Now, there'll be no more talk about it."

Mr. Zibilich walked out.

No sooner had he left when Annie was served with legal papers. She was being sued by one Emma Rose Brewer who'd tripped over the wine bottles on her exodus from the shop on the day of the book discussion debacle, breaking an arm and leg.

And so Zella, noting a pall had settled over the back room in the wake of these discoveries, that Leo had slipped into a funk as he lay supine on the cot while she fed him chicken noodle soup, that Annie could barely lift her head after gazing at the legal papers, tried to boost everybody's spirits by starting a conversation.

"Ain't nobody ever accuse me of being superstitious," Zella noted. "But do you know what day it is? Friday the 13th. Let's go 'round the room, tell 'bout the worst day of our lives."

"Now why," Annie groaned, slumped in a folding chair next to the cot across from Zella, "would you think it important to be reminded of that?"

"'Cause it'll cheer everybody up, Annie Blue." Zella, raised in the Mississippi Delta, had taken to calling Annie that, saying she complained so much about her lack of customers it was like she was singing the Delta blues. Zella lifted a spoonful of soup; Leo raised his head. He opened his mouth; she spooned it in. "If nothing else it'll remind us of the days we went through a whole lot worse than this. Now, you go first, Leo. Tell it like it is, baby."

Leo closed his eyes and swallowed. "The day I was sentenced to federal prison," he croaked. He lay back down and shivered.

"Now you, Annie Blue." Zella pressed the tip of a cracker against Leo's bottom lip. He bit it off and chewed.

"No. You, my dear."

"Okay. I'm next. The day my chil'ren die." Zella put down the broken cracker, twisted the wrapper, and shrugged. "There ... that's 'nough. Now you."

Zella slid an arm under Leo's shoulder and raised him. The steam lifted from the soup as she spooned it in his mouth. Annie wondered how many times Zella had performed this ritual with her kids and grandkids over the course of half a century. Because of the lingering cold, Annie had let Zella and the boys continue sleeping in the shop. It was either that or return to their freezing shotgun double where the boys might catch pneumonia and Zella break down from the strain of it. She couldn't take that chance.

She'd seen it, Zella pointed it out, the little house on St. Andrew Street not far from the abandoned building. It must have been white once but turned gray over time with a door on opposite sides and a window beside each door with shredded curtains behind black metal bars. Zella, Feayo, and Nehemiah lived on one side of the shotgun double, in two tiny rooms and a kitchenette. *Poorest of the poor.* She didn't know much about Zella, only that she'd raised two daughters and two sons, none of whom were alive today; but she was tight-lipped about the circumstances of their deaths. Zella could be blunt about many things, loose and raw and raunchy, but she rarely spoke about her personal life, and Annie didn't wish to pry. She figured all would come out in time. As for herself, she was depressed. She needed to talk.

Leo brushed away Zella's hand and went into a coughing fit. Zella put down the spoon, propped another pillow under him.

Annie's voice was flat: "I do recall thinking, 'This is the worst day of my life.'"

"Keep on talking, baby. Tell ole Zella."

"What would you like to know?"

Zella absently stirred the soup. "Tell a story. What brought it on?"

"So you're into the gory details? Want to savor every macabre morsel."

"Don't know what you mean 'macabre'. But I done tol' you my babies die. Leo tol' you he gone to prison. What could be more 'macabre' than that?" Zella said, offended. "What's wrong, baby?" she went on. "You hiding something bad? Any of your babies die? Anyone throw you in the slammer?"

Zella kept stirring. She bent forward, moving her face toward Leo's. His was chalk-white. His glasses had been smashed during the fall over the wine table and his eyes shone clearly. They were bloodshot, rheumy. Zella placed the back of her hand against his forehead. She turned to Annie. "What's so bad you can't tell ole Zella?"

Annie studied her, got up, and made her way to the door. She stared into the front room. She turned back to Zella.

"I killed my husband."

Zella's spoon, half lifted, tilted. Soup spilled over Leo's covers. She put the spoon back in the bowl, set the bowl on the floor. She took out a napkin, dipped it into a glass of water, and delicately wiped the spots. She looked up at Annie. "Why don't you come back, sugar? Come back and sit here with ole Zella."

Zella's lips were slightly parted.

"We were going to Ocean Springs, Mississippi …" Annie began, returning to the room. She stood looking down at Leo, watching the movements of his chest. His mouth was open; he was snoring. "… to have dinner at my cousin's bar. It was actually my cousin's husband's bar. He was a retired engineer who'd bought a sports bar as a hobby and he invited us to have supper and watch the Saints game with them. Zack wanted to drive but I insisted."

"I say, why don't you sit down, honey?"

"I never do that," Annie murmured. Hypnotically, she sat down. "I always let Zack drive. He used to drive a cab in the days he lived in Vegas. He was a great driver but lots of times he'd drive too fast. We'd started out late. I thought he'd try to make up for lost time."

Zella looked down at Leo. "'Cuse me, baby." She got up. "I'll be right back." Zella waddled to the bathroom. Annie could hear the medicine cabinet opening. Zella returned, nudged Leo on the shoulder, and patted him on the cheek. She had a thermometer in her hand. She slipped it into Leo's mouth. "Go on, sugar."

"I'm a slow driver," Annie continued, taking a deep breath and letting it out. "By the time we approached the I-10 Twin Span Bridge that crosses Lake Pontchartrain, it had begun to rain. The rain began coming down hard and I could barely see through the wipers. I began to panic. I couldn't see the car ahead. Zack was telling me go faster. I had nearly slowed to a crawl. He was afraid a car would rear-end us."

Annie paused. "The rain terrified me. I couldn't *see*. I wanted to pull over till it stopped. But Zack kept pleading, 'For chrissake, this is how pileups start ... You don't want to go this slow. Keep on ... Go faster ...'

"He sounded scared out of his mind. By now, we were on the bridge. I knew I couldn't pull over. The rain was coming in torrents. It was just my natural instinct to slow down. It was night. It was foggy. The rain was coming in sheets and it was impossible to see. There was a jolt. The car behind us. We were going through the rail. We were in the water ..."

Annie buried her face in her hands. She got up and hurried to the front room. She needed to see her books. She sat at her desk, taking in the rare, autographed, and first editions. Her eyes roamed to the 'Southern Literature' then to the category, 'Great writers who killed themselves,' kinky but original, then to a small bookcase labeled 'Fabulous books for cheap,' a grouping of all her torn, dirt-smudged, written-on personal books she'd read at least a dozen times, special among them William Kennedy's *Ironweed*, her second favorite novel.

It was peaceful where she sat; she felt comforted and emboldened. Then her worries began again, the realization she had not one single customer. She thought about the civil suit and how she hadn't taken out liability insurance and would have to find a place to live if her business were to survive. Of course, if she had to pay a court judgment — and the cost of living somewhere else and there was little money coming in because she was hardly making any sales — she'd surely have to call it quits. She'd been in business less than two months. How could everything go wrong so fast? She'd allowed for no margin of error. She knew when she first opened she was making potentially fatal errors. She'd simply refused to listen to her better judgment.

She'd feared if she waited for all the conditions to be right, she'd never open up shop. And this was her last chance to redeem a life increasingly grown desperate. She knew she hadn't started with enough operating capital. The American Booksellers Association advised starting with at least $250,000 before even opening one's doors. Anything less would be suicide in today's competitive market. Yet, she'd started with barely $50,000. And she knew the location was wrong. People here were poor. Location was *everything. Everything. Everything.* Two fatal mistakes.

She got up and went back to sit with Zella.

"It's all right, baby," Zella cooed. "This dumb broad down stuck her big foot in her mouth. You don't wanna talk, you don't gotta."

Zella turned to Leo. The thermometer lay on a side table. "You burning up, sugar. Annie and me, we gotta get you some help." Zella tried rousing him. "Come on, we taking you to Big Charity."

"Hell, no." Leo shoved her hand away.

"You on fire, sweetheart."

"You're not taking me there."

Annie went to the fridge, removed a carton of orange juice, and poured the juice into a glass. She opened the freezer, took out some ice cubes, and deposited them inside a washrag. She returned to her chair, pressed the folded rag against Leo's brow. Zella took the rag from her and patted his face. Leo had been complaining of a headache. Now he was practically too weak to talk. Annie took his hand, wrapped it around the glass. "Here," she said softly. Leo struggled to lift the glass. His glands were swollen, his face swollen. He was having trouble swallowing. His skin was turning greenish-gray.

"Leo," Annie whispered, still supporting his hand. "I don't know how to take care of you. I don't even know what's wrong. Please ... we need to get you to Charity."

"No." He shoved the glass away.

"Them docs gone fix you up, sugar," Zella said cheerfully. "I know them docs. I done give birth there four times."

"Yeah," he said hoarsely. "You and I were on different floors. I was in the de-tox ward and I'm never going back."

"It's all right," said Zella. "I done took care of worse." She pressed the palm of her hand against Leo's chest to ease him down and soon he was fast asleep. Her attention turned to Annie. "So your car went through the rail? You in the drink? Some car rear-ended you? You don't have to talk about it."

"No, no, it's okay." Annie glanced into the front room. "I always knew he was a hero ..."

"A hero?"

"Zack." Annie looked back at her. "My husband saved my life. We were going down into the lake, I couldn't get my seatbelt off. I was panicking, it wouldn't release. Zack got it unbuckled. He began opening the sliding window on the roof — the moon roof, they call it — and that's how I got out. I was rising to the water's surface, about to explode because I couldn't breathe. And when I got to the surface, Zack wasn't there."

"Oh Lawd …"

"It was me, the water, the pounding rain. Freezing. And it was dark. Zack wasn't there. I went down again to get him. I couldn't see. And then I saw him. He was floating in the back of the car, against the rear window. I'd have to go through the moon roof to get into the back. Close spaces panic me. I was scared of being trapped back there. I tried opening the door but couldn't. I couldn't hold my breath."

"No one could …"

"I reached the surface, gasping. A man, I later learned, a former Marine, dove into the water. He got me out then the paramedics came and divers. They tried saving him. It was too late. I should never have left him. I know he'd never leave me."

"It weren't your fault."

"He got disoriented, lost his capacity to breathe, wasting time with me. He didn't have much breathing capacity. He smoked —"

"It's all right."

"It's not all right!"

"Don't talk about it no more."

"Insisting on driving. Going too slow. Trying to pull over. Leaving him —"

"Shut-up, you don't have to say nothing!"

"I should never have left him."

"It's done. Can't take it back —"

"And when I went back down, I should have gone in and got him. He'd still be alive today. *I didn't even try —*"

"Can't take no more of this! Didn't mean to start this shit!" Zella was beside herself, reaching down for her foot and raising it to the cot. She took off her slipper and rubbed her toes hard. "You stop beating yourself to death," she cried. "You done the best you could." She put her slipper back

on, picked up Leo's bowl and dumped the remains in the garbage. She sat the bowl in the sink, picked up the box of crackers, put it in a cabinet. She took out chocolate chip cookies and placed them on the card table. It was nearly three o'clock. The boys would be getting home soon. She sat down, looked at Leo. She reached over, took Annie's hand.

"How long ago this happen?"

"Five years."

"And the other car? The one rammed you?"

"He got lucky. A few broken ribs. No one else in his car."

Zella made her way to the sink. She began putting dishes away. She was mumbling, head bent, trying to put what she'd heard behind her, saying over and over without looking at Annie that everyone makes mistakes, it was done, it was over, and she'd done the best she could, no one was perfect, no human 'cept Father Seelos, why she herself made mistakes, turning at that point to gaze, stricken, down at Annie.

"I done stuff you wouldn't believe," she said. "And I ain't judgin' nobody for what they did. I raise four babies and none of em turn out right. We all make mistakes, baby, but we jus keep on keeping on."

Zella had turned around, clinging to her dishrag. "You jus do the best you can and God'll take care of you." She turned fiercely back to the sink, began banging dishes around, washing them, slapping them on the counter. "You wanna talk about mistakes?" she said, whirling around angrily. "I was a working girl in my day. Oh, I never call myself a whore. I call myself a *professional* ..."

Hands on hips, balancing her weight on one foot then the other, she continued: "I begun when I was sixteen. In them days, I wanted to be a *professional* — chief executive hooker — boss lady of the big bed with plenty of sugar in my pocket. It sounded good in them days, and that's how I lived my life. Whore on the street. Big, fat sassy whore. Not doing nobody harm, that's what I tol' myself, not knowing what the Lord had in store for me, and over the years I had babies. Raise em all myself. Why, I was so busy being a *professional*, I didn't have no time for them. Destroyed my babies' lives. They was running the streets, ragged, and every one of em die young. You talk 'bout a soul never had no sense ...

You think *you* done wrong? Everything I done was wrong. 'Cause the kinda lives they choose to live, I was responsible for."

"Listen —"

"No, *you listen.*"

Zella placed her hand over her heart before tossing out the rag. She reached for a towel, dried her hands and grabbed Annie's hand. "Ain't no use talking — *come on!* " Zella headed for the front room. "You and me," she bellowed, dragging Annie along, "we got *business* to tend to."

She waited long enough for Annie to lock the door before rushing her up Magazine to Josephine and hanging a left. Charcoal gray clouds hung in the sky as men idled outside a corner building across the street from St. Mary's Assumption Church. They were murmuring to one another, drinking beer in brown sleeves. They peered up at the clouds then at Annie, whose hand was attached to Zella's, as the old woman led her to the great mahogany doors.

When they entered the church, Zella led her down a center aisle. She opened an interior door to the right of the high altar and entered a room. Inside was a shrine, a museum of sorts, with portraits on walls and newspaper clippings encased in glass. Appearing in front of a wall directly opposite the door was a life-sized bronze statue of a man, the same image as in the portraits. The man looked to be in his mid-forties. His forehead was broad, his hair wavy, the look in his eyes intense — intelligent — behind small wire-rimmed glasses.

It appeared to Annie as though he were staring straight at her, not judgmentally but with kindness and good humor. He was handsome, resembling the movie actor Warren Beatty except he was a man of God. He held out a crucifix. At the base of the statue was the legend, "Cheerful Ascetic."

Zella genuflected before the statue and got down on her knees. She motioned Annie to do the same. "Annie Blue," she said, looking up. "Seventeen thousand tourists visit St. Mary last year and it all 'cause of him. Blessed Father ..." She folded her hands, looked reverently into his eyes. "I'd like you to meet Annie. Annie, this is Francis Xavier Seelos.

"Father," Zella continued, her voice gentle and adoring. "All your life you love the poor and people who been abandoned. Right now, we need you. We don't know what to do and we asking for your help. As you know, I got them boys and Annie here, if she give up, our asses gone be on the street again. And Annie she got her own problems. She can't stop wallowing in her shit. She don't know how to take the day and make something special outta it. She make herself sick, despising herself. You gotta do something." She stared silently, an urgency coming over her. "Get her through this, Father, so she can concentrate on *business*. She hard up for cash. She gotta figure a way to get more.

"And you and me," she said devotedly, "we both know the shop gone take care of us. But Annie, she don't know it. She gotta figure a way to get more customers. She so busy wallowing in her shit she can't come up with a plan. Help us. We counting on you. Leo, most of all. He's sick and drinking hisself to death and ain't got no purpose in life. Put on your thinking cap and give us your best advice."

With enormous effort, Zella got to her feet. She looked reproachfully down at Annie. "I'm leaving," she said sharply. "You stay here and give me the keys. I'll take care of your customers. You stay long enough and keep an open mind, he'll give you some ideas. I been doing this long time. He ain't *never* let me down."

She snatched the keys and shuffled off.

Annie stared in amazement as Zella vanished with her keys. Her first impulse was to chase after her, regain control of her shop. She'd never before been this careless, letting strangers take over, sleep in her place of business, wait on her customers, not to mention handle the cash. It was crazy. And yet for some reason she trusted Zella and respected Leo and believed in the boys and so she stayed right where she was, remaining on her knees.

On her knees, her mind wandered to the days following the accident. She'd excoriated herself, despised herself, feeling an unbearable shame. No excuse was acceptable, so self-loathing she wanted to kill herself, thinking about what she'd done to Zack, waking up with her horror and fighting it day by day till time eventually dulled the pain and her thoughts turned to other things: her dream, the shop.

But the memories never completely went away, no matter how much time passed. And as the scene replayed itself, trying to coach herself inside the moon roof, there was never an instant of forgiveness for what she had not done. If only she could find the courage to put an end to everything, throw herself off the Mississippi River bridge, everything would be dandy. Except what would happen when she woke up after death to find her life even worse than before?

Coward staring up at him. He was smiling down on her, holding out the crucifix, and bestowing on her his kindness. *Father, tell me what to do* ... So many years ago when the dream had seemed reachable, she'd created a business plan filled with good intentions: to ferret out unknown writing talent from unlikely segments of the community: public schools, prisons, homeless shelters, nursing homes; to hold a high school series in which students might write stories and compete for prizes, or where inmates might do the same or the old and destitute; to instill a love of writing in a generation that was far too familiar with sitting in front of a TV screen or escaping into drugs. She would have writing contests, autograph parties, readings to mark special occasions. In her business plan she'd written: "These events will be aimed at showing people that art is something to be proud of and lived for and that a love of literature is an addiction worth pursuing and that the era of great fiction is a million years from dead."

With these events, she'd lure folks into her shop. She'd make it available at night to twelve-step groups and fiction workshops and any social, political and environmental group in need of a free meeting space. If she did all these things, surely someone would buy a book. She'd forgotten about all of that. So sick was she with morbidity she'd forgotten how to hope. She looked up at Seelos and he stared brightly back. She remembered Zella telling her that Seelos needed just one more proven miracle to be canonized a saint. *Don't you worry, Father. That day will come!* For she had suddenly remembered hope. She crossed herself and got up.

IV. glorious in my heart

A Spanish song played on the radio. Zella Theophile could feel her legs and hips sway, and soon she'd be working the floor, for she knew how to do it, shimmying them shoulders, poking out them tits and swinging them big hips like she was a young girl again. Why, all she had to do was stretch out her arms and swirl and she'd be having herself a grand ole time.

Zella smiled as she stood before the window watching the smear of gray cloud press into the powdery white swirls. A tiny bird far up in the heavens glided here and there and disappeared the moment she blinked and looked away. A Spanish ballad replaced the other song and her heart swelled as the passionate and gentle lyrics in a language she didn't understand floated into the room while a hard rain pounded the streets. Men sat on ledges and talked under overhangs but no one was visible on the wet sidewalk on this most gorgeous of rainy days — glorious in her heart for she was delirious with joy over what Francis Seelos had done; there could be no other explanation for the rush of happy news.

The rain came in fierce, driving sheets and bounced off the streets in cute white fingertip patterns. The sky was run together in a solid gray-white. No book customers today in this quickly building downpour. But soon. And she was filled with gratitude because Annie had come back from her visit with a plan. Oh happy happy day. The beat quickened on the radio and she found her shoulders lift and hips gyrate. *What must someone think if he was to look through that window and find this fat ole lady dancing?*

Why, she'd have to tell him the truth: Annie'd come back from St. Mary's with a few ideas to kick around. What would you think if we gave a short story contest with prizes for the winners, she asked? And the stories will have a Mardi Gras theme, and we'll plan it for Fat Tuesday. We'll have to get off our butts this minute and get the announcements out today because we only have eleven days to do it and that's not near enough time. We'll mask and dress in costume and have a celebration afterwards. And we'll have a poetry reading for St. Patrick's Day and a ghost story contest next Halloween. And this is only the beginning. For Thanksgiving and Christmas, we'll have fundraisers to give free books to the poor. And every month, our newsletter will spotlight unknown writing talent and we'll have a party for each and every one to celebrate their achievements. And we'll get talented old folk to write our book reviews and professors to host readings for their most gifted writing students and there'll be no end of the ideas this gang of geniuses can come up with.

Zella had her own news. She'd nearly worried herself sick when Leo's fever began to spike. His teeth chattered. He had chest pains and a cough that produced rust-colored sputum. But despite his fuss and protests, she'd got on the phone and called a doc she knew, who'd diagnosed Leo with bacterial pneumonia. He prescribed an oral antibiotic, which Annie gladly paid for, and they'd immediately put him on it. And though it'd only been two days, he'd already begun to rally. And other happy news: despite the horror of the first one, he agreed to lead the next discussion group. He'd done all right the first time. If only he hadn't got drunk and fallen over that table, it would have been a great success. Zella's thoughts about that lunatic who harassed and bullied Leo would put a blush on the face of Seelos. She'd seen it coming, identified the cunt the moment she entered the room. Back in the day, Zella would have known what to do: Grab her by the hair and drag her to the door and kick her sorry ass till she fell flat upon the pavement, good riddance to the snotty bitch. But she'd grown soft in her old age and the misery had played out. Still, Leo was a stand-up kinda guy. He'd agreed to try it again as a special favor to Annie.

And she'd saved the best for last: Zella had found them a place to live. She'd spent so much time in front of the statue of Francis Seelos she was practically a fixture at the Shrine. She always found herself tidying up before leaving and giving worshippers a taste of her knowledge, for she knew practically everything there was to know about the Redemptorist missionary priest, so much so that this very Sunday morning after Mass, the pastor, Father Marcello Rigoli (she'd gone to thank him for the sermon, as she always did following Mass), asked if she'd be the keeper of the Shrine. It seemed the long-time keeper up and croaked on him. And though he couldn't afford to pay her, she was welcome to live in the rooms above the gift shop. That's where the old keeper lived, in the cramped quarters above the gift shop, and this would be her ministry: conducting tours, tidying up, being a messenger for Francis Seelos.

She'd cried and laughed all at the same time, giddy at the invitation, throwing her arms around Father Marcello and squeezing him in a bear hug. Only, she asked one little favor: *could we all shack up together, me and Nehemiah and Feayo and Annie and Leo?* He agreed, if they could all manage to squeeze in. The lodgings above the gift shop had only three tiny rooms, a bedroom, den and kitchen, but if that was what she wanted, those rooms were certainly hers, and he knew Father Seelos up in heaven would be pleased to have them there.

The sound of an acoustic guitar and the sweetest male voice she ever heard pierced her ruminations, simple and fervent, a voice lifting in devotion to the object of his affections, whoever she was. And Zella found herself honoring that devotion, stretching out her arms, the music's passion swelling in her breasts as she swung out her hip and the lower body followed her knee, her hands sensuous and graceful, that hip moving like a hurricane wind following that knee and that graceful hand as if it'd never known arthritis.

The toes of her right foot slid forward, compelling the back foot, her lashes half closed, reliving the voice of her sweet impassioned youth as though time had never made her feeble, coming closer, closer to the child who stood in the doorway, amazed and glorified, that precious, precious boy seeing his grandma come to him, not so much terrified as stunned as she reached out to take his hand, her other resting on his shoulder and beckoning him to dance. *You doing fine, baby, Feayo; you ain't half bad, young man, half liking it, I can tell, you sweet lil' baby boy.* And surely he could see the triumph in her face whenever he lifted his amazed eyes from feet, even getting into it, his own awkward hips jutting out from time to time. Then she took her hands away, shoulders shimmying, hips swirling, flying into the heavens following that solitary bird into the sweet afterlife in this one rhapsodic, unforgettable moment of good news.

V. words of love to Magdalene

Nehemiah stood before the display window watching the flames shoot into the indigo sky, the orange-red streaks surrounded by billowing smoke that rose from the upper levels of the block-long stretch of buildings across the street from where he stood. He heard animal cries coming from the veterinary clinic and kennel across the street and a human shriek from an upstairs apartment. In the dark, he saw a figure run out of a stairwell followed by a white pit bull. The figure, quick and secretive, ran down the sidewalk heading toward a triangular patch of greenery that divided Magazine Street from Sophie Wright Place. It ran into the park and toward the statue of Sophie Bell Wright, before disappearing into the darkness. Nehemiah recognized the figure. He'd never seen Feayo run this quick before, the white pit bull escaping behind him and taking off in the opposite direction, looking like a ghost in the middle of the empty street.

"Valerie … Valerie …" a voice cried out. Screams and fire engines and more than a hundred firemen. He saw folks stretch out their arms as firemen passed along the animals in burnt and howling bundles. *Where he running? What he doing there?* Nehemiah kept watch as the others gathered at the window. Feayo was never the type to be at the head of things. As long as he'd known him, though they'd spent a lot of time apart, Feayo with Grandma Zella and Nehemiah at his mama's place, he'd been slow and plodding, avoiding anything that had to do with motion, something scared within him protecting himself from exposure. Some folks, Nehemiah knew, dreaded getting out of bed while others rose to the occasion even before the sun came up. And yet, here was Feayo scrambling out of that stairwell while the entire universe slept, frantic and purposeful, defying Nehemiah's expectations.

Grandma and Miz Annie stood before the display window. They ran out into the street, after ordering Nehemiah to stay inside. Nehemiah assumed Feayo snuck out in the middle of the night, rising from the air mattress while Nehemiah slept beside him. Sometime in the middle of the night Feayo must have got up and left the back room where they'd been crashing since the landlord discovered them in the front, and gone to the front and opened the door and crossed the street and broke the lock to the orange door that led up the stairs to the apartments and attic. Nehemiah never knew Feayo to go over there before, mostly avoiding that row of shops that housed the animal clinic and stained glass studio and tattoo parlor and record shop.

He saw bare-feet men in pajamas carrying out howling animals. He saw firemen and fire engines and folks scrambling out of their houses over on Constance Street. The fire was out of control, smoke and water gushing from within. He imagined the terror of those poor animals trapped inside their cages as the fire raged about them. He imagined his own trapped self inside his mama's place and how panicked he'd be with smoke and heat rising.

Nehemiah could hear the night-gowned ladies screaming for the firemen to save Magdalene and Jennifer, the firemen unaware if they were animal or human. He could see men rushing toward the flames, their friends and neighbors trying to hold them back.

"They'll get free if you can just go save them," a woman screamed in the street. "Break open a wall — let them out! *Please* ..."

Others darting up and down the street, searching, holding hissing, squirming cats, carrying them to parked cars.

"Who has seen Valerie, my white pit bull?"

Nehemiah didn't say a word. Feayo's absence didn't go unnoticed. Grandma saying something to Miz Annie before rushing out as fast as her bum legs could carry her to find Feayo as much as anything. *Please let there be a reason.* Knowing better than to say a word.

*

March 20th, the first day of spring.

Roses in the grass in the triangular park. Lilies and daffodils and birds of paradise forming blankets of color, gladioli and marigolds before the statue of Sophie Bell, the saddest poems Nehemiah had ever read, held down by stones here and there among the flowers, words of love to Magdalene and Jennifer and the other thirty-eight animals that perished that Wednesday morning, March 17, 2004. A man dying along with them, trapped in the bedroom above the stain glass studio where it all began before spreading through the other buildings by way of the common attic. The fire was brought under control before morning met noon.

Feayo came home at two the next afternoon.

"Where the hell you been?" Grandma demanded.

Feayo didn't say a word, his eyes empty. (He was that way, most of the time.) And when he did finally answer, his explanation didn't ring true: he'd got up hungering for a candy bar and when there was nothing in the fridge to eat, he'd gone down to the all-night Swifty Serve to get himself some Milky Ways. And because he'd been hungry and it wasn't cold or rainy, he'd sat in the grassy park and ate and fell asleep. Then after awhile — who knows how much time passed? — he heard the screams and saw the flames spit up to the sky. He'd watched the fire from there. Hung around after that. Nehemiah didn't say a word, didn't let the first one slip, some quiet voice in the calmest manner warning him of the danger.

They were alone the next day. Nehemiah had the chance to ask: "I seen you running out that stairwell. What was you doing there?"

Feayo looked at Nehemiah, blinked, and turned away. He headed for the card table; that was where they ate their meals. He stood awkward, looking down. He put his hands inside his pockets, wasting time, stalling, Nehemiah knew, never coming up with an answer, unaware of passing time, lost in his shuffling thoughts, trying to conjure up an alibi, with Nehemiah squirming on the cot.

"Feayo," half pleading, "you can tell *me*." Then in the exploding silence, "What was you doing there?"

Feayo suddenly lifted his chin, looking oddly as if he felt pride. For the first time he didn't seem ashamed or clumsy or faltering, the first time he'd ever seen him looking strong and nearly confident, standing without apology, eyes fixed and assured. For one small moment in time, Nehemiah had something to admire.

"Don't worry, li'l man," Feayo mumbled, leaving without another word.

Nehemiah knew he couldn't dismiss it. If only there was a reason, some noble explanation, for the forty cats and dogs that died. The man that died. The fifteen firemen hurt. Folks without a place to live. The radio hinted of arson. *Wanting to believe. Believe the best in him.* But he could never turn his back on that night and what he no doubt saw.

VI. a path to follow

Grandma at the Shrine. Miz Annie closing out the register. Feayo setting up folding chairs. Leo preparing for the night, after showering and washing his hair and putting on a clean shirt, a brown frayed button-down. His blue eyes shining. The shimmer — light — hadn't often been there. More times than not, Nehemiah thought, Leo's eyes were dull; tonight they shone like stars, his movements light and purposeful as he buttoned up his shirt.

Nehemiah sliced sweet pickles into a bowl of tuna fish. He caught Leo smiling into the bathroom mirror. Nehemiah imagined he'd be excited, waiting for the folks to arrive. It'd been Miz Annie's idea (opposed by Grandma) to have prisoners from the local jail give them their best five-page stories in a contest to be judged by some local writers Miz Annie knew. And the four best stories would be read tonight by their authors. And the listeners by a show of hands would pick the first and second place winners.

"Stupid!" Grandma hooted. "Orleans Parish Sheriff's Office ain't gone let no felons loose."

"They do it all the time," Leo insisted. "This contest will be for those working as community service inmates in the minimum security transitional work center over on South Broad. These prisoners are routinely trusted out in public and accompanied by guards."

"And besides," Miz Annie backed him up, "it all goes with the plan. It's the kind of thing I've always wanted to do: the poor, young, imprisoned, they have their talents too. And maybe with recognition, it'll stir up some dreams for them."

"Bullshit," Grandma snorted. "They prob'ly can't even read. You gotta stop being so … stupid …"

But Miz Annie wouldn't listen. She went over to the Criminal Sheriff's Office to get their permission but they sneeringly refused. She even heard them laughing behind her back. Next day, she tried again. And the day after that. She was trying to wear them down, refusing to give up. She kept nagging them, saying it'll be an "educational" experience for the inmates, something the city can take pride in — the nation — bestowing honor upon the Sheriff's Office; and Nehemiah guessed that got their attention. She returned one day. "They agreed to try it as a pilot program," she giggled. And after that, she made sure four winning entries got picked and the inmates invited to come at eight, to be brought to the shop by guards.

Miz Annie put notices in *The Times-Picayune*, which, smelling a feature story for its *Lifestyle's* section, sent over a reporter to do an interview. A write-up appeared. Miz Annie expected a big turnout.

Leo glanced Nehemiah's way. "What's up? Hey, pal, what's bothering you?"

"I got something I gotta tell you."

Leo came over, pulled out a chair.

"I got up early the morning of the fire," Nehemiah confided, cracking a boiled egg against the side of a bowl. He peeled it, sliced it into the tuna. "I had to go piss and I seen Feayo missing so I went to the front room and looked out the window and that's when I seen the fire."

Nehemiah put down the knife.

Leo, sitting with elbow against table, leaned his cheek against the palm of his hand.

"And when I seen the fire," Nehemiah went on, "that's when I seen Feayo." He dumped a spoonful of mayo in the bowl. "He was running out the door that leads up to them apartments."

"What time?" Leo asked.

"Dunno. Maybe five. Maybe 'fore that."

"Anyone with him?"

"A dog. Pit bull. There wasn't no one else."

Nehemiah stirred the bowl.

"That was a week ago," Leo pondered. "Why didn't you tell me then?"

Nehemiah shoved the bowl to the middle of the table, lifted a bowl of egg shells and the knife and took them to the sink. He put the mayo in the fridge. He reached for a loaf of po-boy bread and placed it on the table. He stacked plates and sat down. "Maybe it ain't nothing? Maybe he was in that building for some good reason? Maybe he was trying to put out the fire?"

The light had faded, replaced by a look Nehemiah couldn't identify. Leo shrugged, placed both hands on the table and, frowning, looked down. He shoved his chair back.

"I tell you what," he said, standing. "We have just enough time to eat before the contest begins. When it's over, I'll talk to him. Don't you say anything. Let me handle this."

*

They came in quiet, lean, inscrutable, wearing the unmistakable patina of bedraggled submissiveness, on their faces a "dull torpor of the soul," James Joyce might have called it, Marvin thought with a cynical smile. Still, he detected a glint of expectancy in them as, sandwiched between guards, they were led to a table where they were told to sit down. Their expressions alone brought back his past, recalling the soporific drip of monotony, which ultimately forced him to a place of refuge in lieu of a slide into insanity. No doubt it would come to that with seven years looming ahead. That, or he'd look just like them, robotic, dehumanized, undistinguishable from anything on earth, as valueless as a cipher except for the sheets of paper they would not let go of.

Who could imagine anybody would come to this? Who'd think human nature was so perverse that a bunch of sorry losers could route them from their homes on a work night out of a need for some oddball entertainment? Marvin could imagine that fun-loving literary types might be drawn to a Mardi Gras reading, complete with King cake and second-lining. But even that hadn't turned out as hoped.

They'd held that fiasco a month ago. Marvin had envisioned the Mardi Gras readings might be well attended, with locals who traditionally avoided the parades coming in decent numbers. Instead, the few who straggled in were drunks from the streets with beads wrapped around their necks and mamas with little kids who'd been to the parades on St. Charles Avenue and were returning home to rest but, spotting the sparkling Randazzo's King cake through the display window, decided to treat their kids to a snack.

Marvin, a perfectionist in all things literary, though a calamity in all things personal, allowed himself to believe that some of the readings might meet his expectations — after all, this was New Orleans where creative people thrived — the works themselves adhering to such literary devices as plot, characterization, conflict and resolution, or, at the very least, showing some familiarity with tension, suspense, foreshadowing, and moral choice.

It had been decided that anyone who wished to participate would be encouraged to read from his own work, the rule being that the author dress in costume. Since they were so late arranging the event, they decided the stories didn't necessarily have to carry a Mardi Gras theme. Rather, the reader could use any story he so desired, as long as the work was of his own creation. But to his bitter disappointment, most weren't even adequate. They weren't even what one would call stories, really, but anecdotes penned by beginners, derivative and soulless. Marvin began to wonder what he'd gotten himself into, why was he even there? He wondered whether anyone with talent would walk into this shop to make these events worthwhile.

And as he daydreamed through one of the readings, his eyes roamed to the street and stopped at the spectacle of a tree. It was across the street. He hadn't noticed it before. A scrawny, puny tree, maybe ten or eleven feet tall, and he didn't know what kind it was or cared, and it didn't much matter anyway. It was barren, without so much as one leaf upon its flimsy branches. And hanging from it were a thousand Mardi Gras beads, in green and purple and red and gold, and they were dangling like peppermint sticks from every single branch, highest to lowest, blinding Marvin with glowing color, dazzling him with their beauty, gleaming and hopeful. A cardboard sign hung from the tree: "Whosoever tries to shake this tree is an asshole."

Could it be a bunch of jokers got together in the drunken night to give Marvin a reason to laugh? And in the act of laughing fill his soul with hope? It came to him there was nowhere else he'd rather be than right here in Annie's shop on Mardi Gras Day waiting for someone brilliant to arrive. He or she didn't have to be brilliant even, but in the act of creating, roll upon the carpet of their waiting lives just one pure moment of insight — a single, subjective truth. And if that didn't materialize, maybe the next event would be better. Who knew? Some unknown with potential might unexpectedly walk in and read something interesting and affecting and blazing with the glow of language, and they would have discovered him or her and the shop would be part of history, like *Shakespeare & Company,* where James Joyce hung out, and they'd clink their glasses in tribute and drink to the voyage of the next great discovery.

It was hope that drove him on. And it was hope that stirred him this night, like a gambler at the poker table, here on the night of the prisoners' readings. He hadn't read all of the entries. In fact, he'd read very few. He'd been busy writing a new novel and penning an ending to the final chapter. It was good. His best effort yet. Still, he had a way to go before the manuscript would be completely finished, lots of revising, polishing and editing ahead, creating some new scenes perhaps; but the first draft was always hardest and he was proud of what he'd done so far. And so, being otherwise preoccupied, he'd left most of the entries for Annie to read.

She'd picked out her favorite twenty and submitted them to the local judges to whittle down to a final four. But one glance at the prisoners, dressed in their bright orange jumpsuits, looking wary and undeserving, all expectation vanished. *You have to have discipline or conviction or passion to write, something in your gut.* He himself was obsessed, working each sentence sometimes for days, refusing to give up till he'd achieved his own perfection. But it was plain there was nothing in the guts of these poor slugs, or, if there was, he hadn't found it.

He was half expecting no one to show at all. It came as a surprise, the numbers drifting in. Enough to fill a bookstore. College kids in jeans. Literary types. Women donning spectacles with hair tied tight in back. Chunky women, lonely. Middle-aged academics. *Emma Rose Brewer has not graced us with her presence, thank god.* But just as that thought emerged, he looked over at the entering crowd to see he'd spoken way too soon.

*

There she was, brace on arm, cast on leg, hobbling, on a single crutch. A pitiful sight. A godawful shocking horrifying sight. And the thought entered his head that someone that reckless as to walk into a crowded event at night in that vulnerable condition, alone, at her age, was clearly seeking trouble. How on earth did she get here? Who brought her? Surely, someone brought her. No way could she drive herself. So how the fuck did she get here? And why? Marvin hurried over to help, make sure no harm came to her, find her a place to sit. This shop didn't need another Emma Rose disaster.

And as he moved to get to her, he was nearly knocked over by Zella, a ferocity in her vengeful eyes, fists clinched, chin out. Zella almost blitzkrieged him in her haste to get ahead, beat him to the punch. She was rushing straight toward Emma Rose. Marvin knew Emma Rose, of course. He and Annie had many a chuckle, trying to make light of the calamity that descended upon the shop almost immediately following her arrival at the inaugural discussion. They'd cracked their jokes, had their fun, even after Emma Rose filed suit, but Zella took it personally, mumbling she had every intention of cleaning that bitch's clock if she were so unfortunate as to run into her again, spread her disgusting lard all over Magazine Street for the pigeons to peck at, get even in the name of Annie.

And so Zella was rushing to her with dizzying speed while Marvin hustled to reach her first. Too late. Zella already had her hands on Emma Rose. Emma Rose, looking terrified, was surrounded by the stunned gathering, their faces grim, appalled, watching with stark curiosity, too fascinated to bother to lift a finger to help. Marvin knew what was coming. One push would send her sprawling, shattering into brittle bits, into a thousand brittle pieces, for Marvin to clean up, of course. He prayed for intervention, for someone to save the night, at least save Emma Rose.

They stood gawking, immobile in their close space, the fear of God in the eyes of Emma Rose (he couldn't see Zella's face), Zella holding on to both shoulders, standing in evil stillness as if she'd been zapped by some extraterrestrial, her rigidity more than odd. Marvin cringed. Emma Rose was turning scarlet. She'd begun stuttering, pleading. "Listen to me ..." she hollered, "... I ... I have something urgent to tell Miss Ajami ..." but Zella was bellowing, "Shut the fuck up, bitch, you ole douchebag ..." and "get your fat ass out that door *right now* ..." applying pressure on the shoulders, nudging her to turn around till Emma Rose faced the entrance door.

But not before Marvin saw horror in the eyes of Emma Rose. She was frantic, searching desperately for one last chance to find a certain party — Annie — Marvin could tell, to intercede in her behalf. He kept trying to reach Emma Rose, save her, because it was clear she was being ejected, the gathering separating as she passed. Awkwardly, she maneuvered her crutch, edging forward clumsily, while Zella continued applying pressure. And that's when Zella kneed her in the butt, hands pressed to the shoulders so that it was impossible for her to fall, till she stood solidly on the sidewalk, the door slamming behind her. A wicked grin. Zella slapped her hands in victory, waddled past the bloodless crowd beyond Marvin and the folding chairs, to vanish through the back door as swiftly as she came.

Everybody seemed stunned. An instant of embarrassment. Then an old man walked through the door, the one from the inaugural crowd, patting Marvin on the shoulder before taking a seat in the front row. The prisoners at the table glanced hollow-eyed at the old man. People began moving, doing whatever they were doing before, as Marvin took his seat at the table, in the empty chair, with two prisoners on either side. Guards leaned against the wall, no more than a few feet from their charges, and the readings began.

*

Marvin breathed a sigh of relief, gathered his strength to face the night. More guests were arriving, heading for the refreshment table to fill their glasses with wine and plates with cream cheese balls before settling into folding chairs and chatting with one another. Marvin watched. He despised public speaking. Sociability had jarred him ever since he was a child, his greatest pleasure taking pencil to pad and making tangible his roaming thoughts in deepest solitude.

But in this, his thirty-ninth year, more was to be expected. Life no longer was for doing whatever he wanted; it was for doing what was before him. AA taught him that.

It was for putting one foot in front of the other and doing the next right thing. Emotions played no part in it. It didn't have to feel good. It only had to *be* good. It was asking a Higher Power to communicate His will for him and then be willing to do it. He was willing. He'd started going to meetings when he had been in prison. Then, when he got out and began drinking again, he'd only managed to go a few more times. Once or twice he'd walked in drunk. But nobody cared. They were grateful he'd shown up at all, thinking one day he'd get back on the wagon. But that had never materialized. And he hadn't kept up with meetings, not that he didn't find them valuable and the characters amusing at times.

He'd long ago stopped following the Steps. Didn't do a damn thing that would bring peace to his life. One by one, most of the promises he'd made had been broken. But that didn't mean he didn't *want* to do the right thing, whenever the opportunity presented itself or whenever he found the courage. And what his Higher Power was telling him now was as clear to him as anything on earth: give these prisoners a shot. A glimpse of something. A path to follow. Open up a door.

Besides, Annie had asked a favor.

So he was willing. And yet there was more to it than that. Even if his Higher Power hadn't whispered in his ear, he knew his actions tonight were right on a different level. He had agonized for some time, *What is it I can do that is decent and honest?* He'd dug himself into a hole over the course of many years and now there was no getting out. Be an investment banker? Doctor? Lawyer? Chemist? Engineer? These careers were lost to him, thanks to his foolish ways.

No one would hire an ex-con. And he was too old to go back to school, didn't want to anyway. But he could write. And he could read. He'd nearly won the most prestigious prize in his field. Annie needed him in this

endeavor, and he certainly could oblige. He could be useful.
He'd host her events, she'd be successful in time. He'd be
her employee, earning enough to get by, making it possible
for him to do the only thing he had ever wanted to do:
write.

That was the plan.

And so looking out upon the crowd, Marvin prayed
no harm would come. He was worried that when the
prisoners began to read, the listeners would lose interest and
find their way to the door. And then the night would be a
failure and so would Annie's shop. To his surprise, the first
three readings met with genuine appreciation and applause.
Then something happened that shocked him. The
scrawniest of the prisoners — a youth of twenty-one with
brown hair and hazel eyes and a hard, stark look and acne
scars and tattoos — stood up when it came his turn. He
spoke barely above a whisper, though it wasn't from
shyness, Marvin knew; he just wasn't used to public
speaking, until someone from the back of the room
demanded he speak up. There was a moment of outrage (his
seething eyes told Marvin) and then his attitude completely
changed, deciding not to embark on his normal course of
action, which would surely get somebody killed, but instead
to go along.

And so he did, raising his voice haltingly at first then
with profound and mesmerizing authority as he fell prey to
his own imaginary world, luring his listeners to a distant
terrain, swept away into a world of the rural Southwest, a
place of mesas and desert mountains and alpine tundra,
where ranchers and cowboys faced bad men with guns,
idealists pitted against psychopaths, unwilling to forfeit their
integrity to save their own lives, bound together in struggle
and cruelty and death. All in five pages that grabbed the
listeners by the napes of their necks and dropped them
before a dust devil, there to witness its calamity and human
carnage and the workings of the human heart. And when it

was over, when this twenty-one-year-old had finished, they sat in amazed silence. The old man was the first to rise. He stood with arms raised, clapping loudly and passionately, the others following in his lead. Every listener in the room left vulnerable by this young man.

The prisoner — Reed was his name — watched calmly and with dignity, poised beyond his years, as if the applause and cheers happened every day. Apparently, he believed in miracles. He had not been surprised. Less jaded than Marvin. And it was this one moment that reaffirmed in Marvin the possibility of things. The opportunities that lay ahead. They needed him and Annie needed him. And Nehemiah and Zella. And Feayo, most of all. He felt giddy and light headed with all the promise the future held, accepting thanks and handshakes from the glowing, departing guests. And after Marvin watched them leave, he saw Feayo folding chairs and stacking them in a corner. *Do you see what you can be? All things are possible.* But Marvin knew better than to say that. It was for Feayo to discover.

Marvin sat back down and dared to hope it would work out. He called Feayo over. "Stop messing with those chairs. Come over and rest your butt."

Feayo finished folding a chair. He sat a seat away from Marvin at the table. Marvin leaned toward him. "I saw you the morning of the fire," he said. "Why were you running out that building across the street?"

VII. a thing in common

Grimly, Feayo turned away. Marvin could hear Zella's flamboyant voice rounding the corner toward a punch line. She, Annie, and Nehemiah had gone into the back room. Marvin didn't suppose Zella would ever stop yakking about her dust-up with Emma Rose. Shrieks of laughter and then everything quiet.

Feayo fidgeted, averting his eyes. After a moment of indecision, he jumped up from his chair, made his way sullenly to the entrance door. Marvin followed, quickening his step, and, after catching up, grabbed him by the arm. "Come back," he demanded. "We've got things we need to talk about."

Feayo did as told, making his way grudgingly till he stood behind the chair, gripping the back of it. The boy's facial muscles tensed.

"Listen," Marvin said, sitting down, "I've got to know. What were you doing there?"

Feayo shrugged.

"That door was always locked. How did you get inside?"

"It ain't always," Feayo mumbled. "Sometimes it ain't."

"Somebody left it open?"

"Dunno."

"What were you doing there?"

"I wasn't. You musta seen somebody else."

"*You,*" said Marvin. "*I ... saw ... you, Delfeayo.*"

Miserably, the boy glanced his way then turned his head toward the wall. He shifted legs.

"Tell the truth," Marvin insisted. "Maybe you were looking for something?"

"No."

"What were you doing there?"

Feayo's jaw jutted out, his bottom lip quivered. He seemed about to say something — a defiant word, a declaration of sorts — but released his grip on the chair and moved dully to one of the folding chairs that hadn't been put away. He fumbled with it, dropping it, and, unnerved by the clamor, stood awkwardly, hesitating, before fleeing like a trapped dog to the entrance door again. Marvin let him go this time. When Feayo was several feet from the door, Marvin yelled, *"Stop ... "* It was a command — unequivocal — one Feayo didn't defy. He stood uncertainly, head bowed, facing the door.

Marvin got up, but instead of going to him, turned the opposite way. "You and me," he said, pacing, "come from different places. I studied at the American School — in Switzerland." He stopped. "You even know where that is?"

He did not wait.

"It's a long way across the ocean ... My old man had money and a good education. He wanted me to be like him. I grew up with both parents. You don't even know what that is."

Feayo, feet apart, stood rigidly without turning. Marvin watched the boy as he jammed his hands inside his pockets. Marvin made his way toward Feayo then put a hand on his shoulder, squeezing. He eased his way in front, facing him, blocking the doorway. "I'm not telling you this because I'm an asshole — I'm trying to make a point. What I'm trying to say" — he lowered his voice — "is that I had all these things, all the things a boy could want to grow up right, and I did everything wrong. I went to prison. You know what prison's like?"

"Yeh."

"You do?"

Feayo did not look at him.

"How do you know?"

"My dad."

"Your dad did time?"

Silence.

"You went to visit him?"

He shook his head.

"How long was he there?"

"Not long ... he die."

"Died jailin'?"

"No."

"I don't understand ..."

Marvin, trying to make sense of it, waited for words of clarity, and in the insistent, unnerving silence, walked distractedly back to the table. He sat down, put his elbows on the table, his face in his hands. He stayed that way for some time. Suddenly he removed his hands and the full force of his gaze rested on the boy's back. "Died trying to escape? Is that what happened?"

Feayo, still with his back to him, turned. As if in a drugged state, he made his way past Marvin to one of the chairs nearest the back room. In the shadows, the chair had been turned around and was next to be put up. Looking dazed, preoccupied, Feayo straddled it backward, crossing his arms against its back. He buried his face in his arms.

"How old were you?" Marvin said softly.

"Two."

"Someone told you about your dad?"

"Grandma ... and there was them ... stories." Looking up, his eyes bore a haunted look. What seemed like grief passed across his face. And almost as an afterthought, "They put my mama in too."

A chime of laughter. In the back room, Zella and Annie were in high spirits, celebrating the night. Marvin could hear the carefree voice of Nehemiah, teasing, cajoling. He turned. "Will you tell me what happened, Feayo?"

Feayo's arms rested against the back of the chair as he stared into the shadows. His voice reminded Marvin of slowly drifting leaves.

"She come to jail, my mama ..."

Marvin leaned forward.

"She sit in a room. Cut the mesh, put a gun on the table. Then leave. He grab the gun, run down the stairs. He threaten a guard if he don't open the door. He run and get in mama's car."

"She was waiting?"

"Yeh."

Feayo's voice remained distant, almost as if he had been hypnotized. And then Marvin heard a noise. It was coming from behind him. He turned around, saw a man at the front door. The man entered the room, started roaming through the stacks. He was wearing filthy boots, leaving tracks all over the floor. He did not look at Marvin.

Marvin's first impulse was to tell him the shop was closed but decided it'd do no harm to let him browse. He would clean up later. He did not want to be interrupted.

"Go on," Marvin said, turning back to Feayo.

The trance was broken. Feayo watched the stranger as he disappeared among the stacks. Marvin pressed on. *"Feayo ... I want to know."*

Feayo hesitated then in a barely audible voice: "He get past the cop cars trying to block the road. Drive fast and they follow."

"Where?"

"I-10. He get off at Vets, sideswipe a car. Pull into a gas station. The cops pull in after him."

"That's where he died?"

"No."

Marvin waited for an explanation, for him to go on. But Feayo seemed lost, disappearing into his story. Marvin drew in a breath. "That's all?" he said, letting it out. "Time to call it a night?" He slid his fingers through his hair, was about to get up when he heard Feayo's raspy voice. The boy's chin was tilted as if looking at the ceiling but his eyes were firmly shut. "He run into a store, tell a woman to lock the door. The woman scared. She try doing what he say but the cops they get in with their guns drawn. Then one runs ahead of the others. He's the one shoot my daddy."

"A cop?"

"Yeh."

"And your ma?"

"In the car. Stay in the car. They charge her with aiding a prisoner's escape, bringing a gun to jail."

"Your Grandma told you this?"

"And I read the stories."

"Stories?"

"In the paper. My Grandma save." Eyes wide open, he was staring at Marvin this time with an intensity that startled him. "She get ten year. But she never serve that kinda time. She was sick. Die 'fore a year was up."

A book fell. Marvin jumped. He turned and saw the stranger, who was picking up the book and putting it back on a shelf before taking out another. The stranger settled in a chair not far from the register. He opened the book, began reading. Zella, Annie, and Nehemiah were calming down in back, Marvin hearing now and then the mellow voice of Zella, probably instructing Nehemiah to get to bed. Feayo remained still, gazing at the floor, utterly alone. Marvin had the urge to comfort him. But his instincts led him in another direction. "Feayo," he said, "have you seen that cop somewhere?"

Feayo looked up.

"Where?"

"'Cross the street."

"Directly across the street?"

"Yeh."

"The cop lives there?"

"Did."

"In the apartment that caught fire?"

Silence.

"How long," Marvin said carefully, "did you know he was living there?"

"Not long."

"How long?"

"'Bout a month."

"You recognized him?"

"Yeh."

"How?"

"The picture."

"What picture?"

"In the paper."

"What kind of picture?"

"He got cop of the year."

"Recently?"

"'Bout a year after daddy die. Big picture. Grandma save it."

"But that was —"

"— He ain't change."

"You set the fire?"

Feayo turned to look at the stranger, who seemed engrossed in the book, too preoccupied to hear anything. And now was not the time to ask him to leave, Marvin thought. "You planned it?" Marvin asked.

The boy's face showed no emotion, but his body seemed to relax. It seemed, tragically, he had grown up too soon, no longer a child, and there was no turning back from the direction he was headed. "Feayo …" Marvin coaxed, "please answer me. You set the fire that killed that cop?"

Feayo did not look away.

But Marvin did. He was caught by the utter stillness in the room, everything as tranquil as morning snow in the place he once lived when he was a boy; by the stranger who had not moved, comical in his obliviousness; the shelves' unflinching rigidity; the books that contained all worlds, as dormant as the walls; the child who could kill animal and human without a stir of conscience. Marvin himself was unable to move, to get up or face what must be done, to probe further in search of some reasonable understanding, for there was none. "Feayo," he said, "you and I have something to do. Do you understand that?"

"You telling on me?"

"We need to tell some people ..."

"I'm going to jail?"

"No, there'll be people who can help —"

"You turning me in?"

"No ... it'll be all right."

Feayo was looking beyond Marvin. Marvin turned, saw the stranger waving the hardback and standing before the counter, as if expecting Marvin to ring up his purchase. Marvin looked at Feayo and then at the man. "I'm sorry," he said. "We're closed." But the man stood looking as if he hadn't heard. Marvin made his way to the counter and was about to say something else when the man — stranger — pulled back his jacket and reached in his waistband. At the same time, he threw down the book. He grinned. "Get movin'," he shouted. "We wasted 'nough time." It was at that moment Feayo moved ahead of him.

It was a flash at first, nothing more than a stir, and then Marvin saw Feayo. He went to stop the boy, hold him back, shield him from the man, but Feayo was moving quickly, heading for the cash register, completely without fear — obdurate, determined. Marvin saw clearly what the man was holding. The man pointed it at Feayo but Feayo didn't care. He didn't even look up. He was so cool and steady and unwavering in his determination that Marvin could only stare and the man stare back, his gun pointed in the boy's direction. Feayo, hurrying, was now behind the counter, pulling out a drawer. The man, apparently hesitant to shoot a child, stood frozen in his spot before swiftly moving himself, running behind the counter, swearing. But he was not quick enough. Feayo pulled out a pistol. The man's gun was pointed at Feayo and Feayo's at him.

All too suddenly, like a car spinning out of control, Marvin could do nothing but stand and watch. And then the muzzle of the boy's gun was aimed in his direction. Like a car that skids, he was seeing everything in slow motion. Marvin saw it clearly and knew what was to come but felt no terror, rather an almost pleasant curiosity, everything vivid and sparkling, the boy's dark eyes staring, an expression Marvin had never seen before, not cruel exactly, but irreversible, so that Marvin knew nothing could save him. He stepped forward and reached out. And in his heart in the final moments was the wonder of it all as to what kind of man he would become.

VIII. father's eyes

Father Seelos had a way with her. His eyes were almost jolly, as if someone told a joke he fully admired, the corners of his mouth turning up to meet the eyes. But there was more to his face that offered consolation: the genuine holiness. How to explain? Annie looked at the statue and knew that she couldn't. Except that the eyes stared back without a trace of judgment, their light bringing peace and friendship and trust. He was handsome as well: the high cheekbones, shapely lips, delicate features, wavy hair. The glasses were what got her — similar to Leo's — and it was that combination of glasses and the intense awareness in the eyes that radiated intelligence; more than that, an uncommon wisdom, and it was the totality of everything that brought a lifting of the heart.

Annie's mind wandered back to the day of Seelos's death, all the stories Zella told her, how the grieving Father Rector ordered Seelos out of bed, not wanting to believe his cherished friend was dying, and how he tried to oblige with all the strength left in him and, failing, and Father Rector, seeing how deeply he suffered, guided him back down and left the room, crying. And later that day, death breathing on him, the priests and brothers crowded into Seelos's room to say prayers and sprinkle holy water.

Zella took such pride in telling the story, how people gathered at St. Mary's before the body was brought in. How during the night, the pews filled with mourners and how a great storm filled the sky so that those who came to view him could not safely go home. How St. Mary's was left open and by daybreak, following the storm, more parishioners drifted in, bringing bibles and rosaries to press against his blessed hand, how they wept and moaned and some even fainted.

Annie wondered what it'd be like to be that loved. She wished she'd known the kind of love that could feel such devastation. She couldn't imagine staying overnight to pray for a dead priest and remain through the morning to be present at his wake, and she imagined how lovely to be part of that community, to love so deeply, grieve so deeply. How honored she was to kneel at the church where the feet of Seelos stepped.

Something told her Francis Seelos couldn't give a tinker's damn whether or not he was made a saint; he was that humble. She wanted to shout in tribute, fling her arms in the air: "Way to go, Father. Way to live a life!" A comfort — joy — swept over her then, a second lifting of the spirit. Dare she think of Jesus on the day of Resurrection? Why, that would be a week from now.

Seelos, she prayed, help me.

She had promised Mr. Zibilich she'd stop crashing in the back. But a promise like that was made to be broken. Surely, she would have kept it if it hadn't been for that night. She'd finished washing her hair, begun drying with a towel, when she heard the gun's report. Zella jumped off the cot with Nehemiah not far behind her and Annie following, the last out the door, when she saw Leo on the floor less than six feet from the register, a stranger's muddy boot peering from behind the counter, the front door open.

Each day we are with you. No one will leave you.

Half each day, she kept company, with Zella taking over. But the doctors had no hope. Neither had she, really. He'd been shot in the head. Of course, Zella had no doubt. Not the slightest hesitation to tell anyone who'd listen that Seelos's intervention would get Leo on his feet and out the doors of Charity and back into the shop, back where he belonged, making a nuisance of himself. And that would be the one miracle to lift Seelos to sainthood. He only needed one. It all made sense. At least, to Zella.

Annie didn't kneel because she believed, didn't look at his jolly face as though he held in his bronze brain the salvation they longed for. Rather, it was only on her knees that a calm came over her and her breathing became regular and the terror ceased, her heart stopped hammering, the dizziness ceased. Or could she hear the healing thought: *take the next right step, perform the next right deed. Try to act honorably, if only for today.* Do not think of yesterday with all its hideous mistakes. Do not think of tomorrow with its consequences derived from yesterday. Think only of today. Seelos constantly reminded her. All she had to do was kneel and look up.

As Annie knelt at Father's feet, peace settled over her. It was dark in the museum and Father's body was draped in shadow. It had rained that morning. New light shone through the beveled-glass to the right of Seelos and through the triangular stained glass high near the ceiling. Everywhere, the floor sparkled. As she gazed to her left, she saw a figure enter the museum and run in her direction, not running in the usual way; rather, the hefty, ponderous body making motions of haste while the swollen feet barely shuffled along, trudging with enormous effort past the holy candles and rosaries, urgently seeking her.

"I done seen him, Nehemiah been talking to him, his face bent to his knees ... He been huddled in the corner of that boarded up house, ain't had no food but what Nehemiah give him ..."

"Wait. Calm down. You're panting, catch your breath."

"Gotta get going, Annie Blue, he may take off any minute, then we'll never see him again ... Gotta get going ... Gotta —"

"Hey, wait. Take a rest."

"Gotta get going, baby girl, get off your fucking knees, gotta get him 'fore the others come ..."

Annie knew better than to argue, knew only to follow as they hurried through the drizzle along Constance Street, Zella's eyes wild. They scrambled to their destination, ignoring the squawking pigeons as they scattered and scurried when they turned the corner to St. Andrew, avoiding the pools of enlarging circles from the rainwater and a mud pile with footprints embedded in the center. As rain tickled her nose, Annie saw the right half of the road was a river of mud-water, dirt-gray beneath a ghostly sky. They reached the last house on the block and stood, panting, in front, staring at the shingled roof and the "No Trespassing" sign. Gasping and heaving, Zella paused to catch her breath.

Not looking at Annie, Zella broke the silence: "I seen Nehemiah taking out food the last few days. I don't say nothing but today I follow. Stay a far distance 'way so he can't see where I am then he go in where the single board used to be nailed 'cross the door, it laying on the ground, the door half cracked. I seen him go in. There ain't nothing in that house 'cept roaches and rats. I don't know how he knowed. I waited then went in. It was dark. I barely seen em in the corner. Nehemiah was bending over him, trying to get him to eat, trying to get him to drink. He was jus sitting with his face buried in his knees. I ain't never felt so sorry …"

Zella's voice choked. She wiped her eyes, took two heavy breaths. She gasped, *"My boys …"* still with that wild and frantic look. She stood motionless for an instant, facing the abandoned building, and then hesitantly stepped forward. With the subtle effluvium of dread, Zella moved wretchedly in its direction as if knowing what was in store for her.

IX. like a demon

Cautiously, Annie followed Zella into the building then tried pulling the old woman back as she nervously crept forward. But Zella would not retreat.

"Baby ..." Zella called out. "... sweet baby ... baby, what's wrong with you?"

"Don't come closer, Grandma."

Zella reached out her hand. Annie stood several feet behind Zella at the entrance to what appeared to be a living room. It was dark, empty of all furniture, eerie with its solitary boarded up window at the far right end of the room facing the fallow ground that would one day become a shopping mall. Zella turned to the voice. A figure huddled in a corner, some fifteen feet to her left. Zella headed toward it.

"I told you, Grandma, don't be coming here ..." Feayo's voice was hoarse. He folded his hands over his eyes, shielding them from the sight of her, then dropped them. "Stay 'way ..."

"You my baby boy ..." — in the sweetest tone — "God help me, sugar, I'll do what I can for you."

"Go 'way. Take him with you."

"Ain't goin' nowhere without you."

Feayo's left hand, nearest the wall, shielded by his raised knees, slowly descended, though it was too dark to clearly see.

"What's that?" Zella murmured.

"Be quiet," Annie warned.

"Feayo," Zella ventured. She was slightly out of breath. "I don't know what went on or why you needs to be here. All I know in this whole world is that I love you to death, darlin'."

"Get outta here, Grandma."

Zella moved forward.

"Grandma ... *goddamn* ..." Another movement of the hand.

"Wait," Annie pleaded. She moved ahead of Zella till she stood in front of her, blocking her path. Nehemiah, sitting cross-legged on the floor not six yards from his cousin, lips slightly parted, could not take his eyes off Feayo, but Feayo's attention was somewhere else. Annie, who'd turned to look at Feayo, saw him staring back at her. She turned and faced Zella.

Annie whispered in Zella's ear, the old woman protesting and Annie insisting. Zella stood rigid, hands clasped, sighing, and then Zella meekly bowed her head. Wordlessly, Zella made her way to Nehemiah, taking her time getting down on her knees, placing her hands on both his shoulders, cheek brushing against his, so that it was wet from where she touched, and she moved her lips to his ear, barely making a motion, and silently he stood up. He helped his Grandma up. They both turned their backs. They moved, stricken, to the entrance door, Zella looking back, eyes gleaming. And then she and Nehemiah were gone.

Annie stood facing Feayo.

"What's the matter, bruh?" Annie said lightly. "You don't like living in my shop?"

Feayo cradled his knees, rocking side to side. He stared blindly at the floor. He stopped rocking, looked up.

Annie tried again.

"You hurt my feelings, Feayo, if you'd rather hang out around here."

Annie's strained smile went unnoticed. Feayo closed his eyes and leaned back.

"Come on, Feayo," Annie argued. "It's time to go home."

"No."

Feayo's voice was muffled. Annie tried again. "Zella and I, we'll fix you the greatest meal. Red beans and rice, as only your Grandma can fix them. And Andouille gumbo, how about that? And devils food cake with raspberry filling and chocolate icing ..." Her lips quivered. "I know you'll want to take a shower." She smiled. "Hell, you can stay in the stall till Jazz Fest, if you like ..."

In his utter stillness, he reminded her of a work of art — an acrylic and fiberglass sculpture she'd seen once at a museum — formed in the shape of a dockworker sitting at a café table, looking so lifelike she thought it real.

"*Please* ..." she begged, "it's time. Or maybe you don't want a shower. We'll still fix the red beans ..."

Across the room, nearest the wall with the boarded up window, a rat scampered across the floor and disappeared inside a hole. Annie's body quivered. Every cell in her body yearned to run away. She forced herself to stay put. She got down on her knees, settled on the floor, and stretched out her legs.

"It's creepy here, Feayo. When can we go home?"

"You go."

Annie's eyes adjusted to the light. She could see how exhausted he looked. She saw something else in his eyes that no one should ever see and her heart filled with pity.

"Are you coming?"

"No."

"Why not?"

"I like it here."

"What's there to like?" Her voice playful.

"The quiet."

"We'll be quiet. We won't ... it'll be like you're by yourself." She waited but no response. "Don't you want to know about Leo? Can you tell me what happened, baby?" Once again, silence. She moved a finger across the floor, sketching a woman's face in profile, a nervous habit since childhood.

And then: "How long you plan on staying here?"

"Ain't gone say it no more. ... *Go home —*"

"You like the quiet," she said. "It's peaceful. A place to rest, I know." She spoke more to herself than him in a voice quietly accepting. She'd grown tired of resisting, tired of persuading. She pressed the fingers of her hand to her temple and sensed that he was watching. "Here is where you don't feel so bad — is that the deal, Feayo?" She rubbed her eyes, letting her fingers slide to her chin before resting on her neck. She stood up, pressing hands to the back of her neck, and rubbed. Breathing deeply, she sat down. "You just want to get away, is that what you want, Feayo?"

"*How many times I gotta —*"

His tone was almost menacing. She pretended not to hear.

"There was a time," she interrupted, "when I couldn't stand being around people." She glanced at the window at the far right wall, two boards nailed across it. "I'd take walks on the worst streets so I wouldn't have to see anyone I knew." She turned. "It's called shame, Feayo. Is that what's bothering you?"

His gaze did not leave the floor.

"Because if it is, you'd better get off your butt and walk out of here right now and show the world you've got guts. Don't apologize for anything because nobody's any better than you."

He was shaking.

"You hear?"

"It's time —"

She'd seen the progression, knew the path, and what she sensed in him frightened her. And then, without warning, she heard rain drumming on the roof and, nearest the spot where the rat had been, water rushing from the ceiling. She wondered if Zella and Nehemiah were outside standing in the falling rain or huddled near the door, listening.

"Feayo ..." she said, and then her thoughts were suddenly empty. She closed her eyes and, in her emptiness, heard her heart wildly beating. She found herself listening to herself, a stranger's forlorn and desolate plea, and feeling estranged from the situation. She thought the stranger's next words unconvincing: "I mean it. Nobody's better ..." Not that she wasn't sincere but the stranger's voice was so detached.

He didn't move, probably wasn't listening, having reached some place she could never go.

"Feayo ..." She stood up.

"You don't know ..."

She was shocked to hear the voice, that there was still a part of him that would answer.

"Don't know what?"

"I killed Leo."

"You ..."

"And the man ..."

"Leo's not dead. And the man, he died with a gun in his hand. Was he trying to rob the place, Feayo?"

Silence.

"That makes you a hero. I knew that's what he was doing. And Leo, he got in the way? You shot him aiming at the man?"

Silence.

"My gun was missing," she said. "I figured you had it. That's my gun behind your knee, isn't it?"

He looked away.

"Honey, I didn't mean to keep the gun in the drawer. I meant —" She stopped, pressing hand against her cheek then putting both hands behind her back. She sighed. "How did you know it was in the drawer?"

Silence.

"So you took it out and fired? I figured it had to be you. I knew the man didn't shoot Leo. His gun was fully loaded. And Leo, he didn't have one. The police figured the distance and direction and trajectory of the bullets in relation to where the two were lying so they knew where the shooter was when the gun went off. The only thing I had to believe was shooting Leo was an accident."

A light shone through the window and quickly went away.

"Let's go home," she pleaded. "We need you ... we can't live without you, Feayo."

Amid the silence, she was aware of constant thunder and rain bouncing off the floor. She wanted to come closer, but his face was arched in such a way she dared not take a step. And then, "It was an accident?" She waited. "Some kind of ...?"

He said nothing and she thought, *this too will go nowhere.* Then before the thought had dimmed, she heard, "I knew he was gonna tell."

He reached down and when his hand reappeared, that's when she saw the gun. He took his time getting up. He walked stiffly, like an old man, stopping a short distance from where she was. "I'm telling you, go home."

"Don't you want to come, baby?"

He stared through her, the muzzle of the gun pointed to the floor.

"What are you going to do?"

He made gestures for her to move toward the door. She moved to the window instead, standing with her back to him. Through a portion of glass, she saw the vista of furrowed land slated to become a shopping mall. She'd read about the development in recent days, that it would contain a 200,000-square-foot Wal-Mart, and there would be a thousand housing units, including 250 for low-income residents, using federal dollars to get rid of the monolithic housing complex that once had been St. Thomas. Sorrow swept through her for everything that must change, wiping away the good, the bad, everything that had come before.

Rain fell in torrents, the sky blackened with streaks of lightening. She was surprised to hear hail. In the distance, thunderclaps. The ground swelled with pools of water. She knew what would happen without him even saying a word.

"I won't let you."

"You ain't got no choice."

"I won't leave you."

"I won't let you stay."

He did a strange thing. Instead of forcing her to the door, he turned, made his way to his old spot on the floor, as if not even this was worth his fighting for. He sat down, lifted his hand, and pressed the muzzle to his head.

"*No ...*"

He looked at her almost tenderly, breaking the cold, exhausted performance she knew was a slide to death. She could see what had been there from the beginning, long before she entered the room, and it was creeping up on her too, damning her with its presence so that she shuddered to cast it away.

She made her way toward him, irresistibly drawn, then, growing scared, walked back to her place on the floor. She sat down, legs outstretched. "What was Leo going to tell?"

As if not even this mattered, he laid down the pistol but did not let go the handle. He leaned back, closing his eyes. "That I set the fire." Then, "'Cause the cop was there."

"Who?"

"The man who kill my daddy."

"The cop?"

"I kill him ... and them animals."

"You knew others were in the building?"

"A thought came ..." His attention roamed to the boarded window, fixing on the nailed-down planks. He stared dreamily, voice cracking, and she could barely make out his words. "I was thinking about getting candy at the

Swifty Serve and it come outta nowhere. And every day, it wouldn't go 'way. I start working out the details, not thinking I was gone do nothing. It was no harm ... empty thoughts ... It took my mind off ... made me feel good ..."

"Setting a fire made you feel good?"

"The thought ... 'cause he was there."

"You weren't going to do anything?"

"Jus a thought ..."

He looked bewildered, closed his eyes. She imagined he hadn't slept in days, and how exhausted he must feel, and wondered if she were to sneak up on him right this minute, take away the gun, would it finally be over? And what would she do once they got him home? Stirring, he looked up.

"What happened to make you?"

"I was doing my homework ... I couldn't work out a problem. Leo, he was out and you was somewhere. I couldn't ask Nat, he wouldn't know, and Grandma ..." He shrugged. "I was getting pissed trying to figure it out — it was math — and I needed it for the next day. If I couldn't figure it out, I wasn't gone get no extra points pull my last test up from an F. I was walking back and forth in front of the window, trying to figure it out. I seen the cop 'cross the street unlock the door, go up the stairs, and he forget to close it. And I don't do nothing ... I couldn't get it outta my ... It was driving me crazy — that open door. Then, late, while y'all was sleep, that's when it ... got done."

"What got done?"

"The fire."

"You make it sound so easy."

"Everything I is, everything I thought I was, it turn out all wrong, Miz Annie. I ain't none of them things I thought I was. I knew I wasn't smart. Wasn't going nowhere. But I never thought ..."

She thought this must be like someone writing a letter before death. In a way he must be relieved to have someone to tell, but she knew this did not change his mind, the thing he planned to do. And then she thought how foolish, she never knew him at all, only the child she thought he was, the slow, sluggish boy she knew now was never him. *It's like people who think they know me but never knew a thing about me.*

"Never thought you'd do what you did? And Leo, he found out?"

"I tol' him."

"That's when you shot him?"

"I was going to jail. Gonna end up the way my daddy ... And then ... it went off."

"You didn't know?"

"Sure I did."

"I don't understand."

"Ain't nobody done it but me, Miz Annie."

"We'll get help."

"Don't need none."

"If you don't, there's no —"

"No way I'm gone live with that."

"Of course, you will. It'll be a thing of the past ..."

To her amazement, he smiled. A myriad emotions crossed his face, and she felt like someone on a roller coaster ride, fascinated and helpless to do anything but watch. She remembered a long time ago she'd been in an auto accident at the top of the Mississippi River bridge, and she saw it coming, saw herself slam into the car ahead, and she wasn't frightened or in the least disturbed, almost as if watching from the window of a passing car. But she could never let this get that far. "Listen ..." she whispered, "you'll be sent to a juvenile home. They'll take good care of you. There'll be people to talk to that can figure it out — the things you don't understand. You'll have a *life* —"

"What life? How many dudes you know offed three men and forty animals?"

"Leo isn't dead. You'll be sent to a juvenile home and only till ..."

He turned away.

"It won't be … What did you *think?*"

His face was bent and she could see his body shake. He released the handle of the gun, put his hands over his face. And all she wanted was to go to him. But she hesitated and, in that moment, that's when he picked up the gun.

"We love you, Feayo."

Then everything changed.

Gone from him was every trace of sadness. He seemed almost composed, decided might be a better word, intractable in his decisiveness.

"I'm going to get your Grandma."

The light had faded to several darker shades and she could no longer see what was in his eyes. She felt her heart race and she didn't have much time. She lowered her head, tried to think of something to say, but a numbness that felt like drowning this time, a drowning in one's sleep, where your arms and legs don't feel a part of you, and she felt like screaming and the impossibility of that, but she knew she must do something. A cry — whimper — and then she heard him say with the most tender longing, "What do you want?"

"To *hear* me … *hear me*…"

"I dreamed I was in the 'dome and run a eighty-four yard touchdown and all the people stood up and cheered for me." He made his way to the window. "Then when I woke, that same old feeling: I was dumb, not good for nothing. Ain't nobody in the world gone cheer for me."

"I will and your Grandma. And other people too —"

He was looking out the window, far into the field. "Myself kill three dudes, don't give a shit about it. Light a fire in a building and go eat a candy bar. Like a demon took over and did what I'd never do if I had some say in it."

"When I was young," she said, "I wanted to be special. And then one day I looked in the mirror and there staring back at me was a fifty-one-year-old fool. A woman

who never amounted to much. But you get over your ...
disappointment ... and do the best you can. And here's the
thing, Feayo: you fall and get up. I'm not saying that's *all*
life's about. *But you fall and get up.* The only thing important,
that really matters, is courage. Not that you're a 'success' —
some idiot football player earning a million bucks. But that
you fall and —"

"What do you want?"

"You asked me that before."

"You ever want nothing?"

"A bookstore ... and got it. To be married and got
it. For a while anyway. And now ..." She shrugged. "What
about you?"

"Nothing"

"Bullshit. You want to play ball. We'll work on it,
Feayo. Work on that dream ..."

"Where? Prison?"

"I told you — a juvenile home. You'll stay till you're
21. You've got to pay a price. I know about prices. I left my
husband to die. Fought my way out of the water and left
him there to drown. And now I have the rest of my life to
think about what I've done. I could have shot myself, taken
the easy way. But that's never going to be an option. Life
goes on. And one day you wake up and give yourself a
second chance. You can't give up, Feayo. There's a demon
in all of us. But there's something else as well. And I didn't
turn my back on it. *Don't you turn your —*"

"Nothing ever turn out right."

"Bullshit and you know it!"

"How I'm gone —?"

"You do, that's all. I remember things I did a million
years ago, things everybody else surely had forgotten, but
they come back with such force they turn your head around.
You *do!* You just pick yourself up and do the best you can.
And make a life, Feayo ..."

"The one you got's better than what you had? You 'bout to lose your shop and you ain't got no husband."

"But I've got the shop. And I've got you and your Grandma and Nehemiah. You know what else? Leo will be coming home. And we'll have Leo back again. And maybe we'll lose the shop. But we'll just get another. And maybe Leo won't be what he was. But we'll take him any way we can. We'll take him upside down and sideways, take him crawling on his belly. You accept what is and you do what you can and that's all it takes ... to make a life. You're young. You don't understand happiness. Your Grandma and I'll teach you. We've made enough mistakes, we've learned a trick or two. Here, let me get your Grandma ..."

"No."

"Feayo ..."

Zella stood in the doorway, holding Nehemiah's hand, her dress completely soaked. Annie looked at Nehemiah, grim but on alert, staring at a spot a few yards from his cousin. Zella squeezed Nehemiah's hand and her voice was shaky. "Baby," she cried, "I come in from the rain and couldn't help but hear. I got something I gotta say."

"Go home, Grandma."

"Yeh, but ..."

"Take him and go home."

"I got something ..."

"Go home!"

"A minute, please. I promise, on Seelos' grave, *jus give me one goddamn minute!*"

Feayo walked back to his corner and leaned against the wall. He didn't look at his Grandma. Zella lifted her chin. She gave Nehemiah's hand a squeeze then drew back her shoulders. Her voice was robust: "Son, sometimes when you got nothing, the only thing you got is Him."

He groaned.

"I know you don't wanna hear it, but He *speaks*, baby boy. To me, He speaks. And it come through Father

Seelos. Maybe not in words. Sometimes when I wanna die, I pray to him. I kneel before his statue, not so much thinking 'bout nothing, then something hopeful come to mind. And it weren't me put it there. Most times, I ain't got one good thought in my head — but *something* put it there. And I know it's Father Seelos."

Zella glanced at Annie as if emboldened by her words, looking hopeful, almost cheerful, and then back again at Feayo. She drew herself up. "I'm *sure*," she went on, "it's Seelos — speaking from the Father. I be kneeling there, discouraged, thinking all them things gone wrong, all them things I'd do different given half a chance, thinking what I done to my own babies when they was growing up, 'cause I didn't have no sense, didn't goddamn know no better, and how they all growed. You know, your daddy gone to prison 'cause he deal in dope. Nehemiah's mama hooked on methamphetamine. So you know what kinda ma they had. And all the rest, but I didn't tell you 'bout the others, Darryl and Mary Clare.

"Darryl was little more than your age — Mary Clare, his younger sister — when they rob a Quarter bar down on Dauphine Street, shoot a barmaid in the head. It was Darryl pull the trigger, I ain't got no doubt 'bout it, 'fore they took off in a stolen Mercedes heading down Tulane Avenue to the I-10 ramp with the cops right after em. You see, the cops, they heard the shots. They started chasing em in their car all the way to the twin span going 130 mph, and, right after they got off the twin span, that's when the Mercedes blew a tire and Darryl lose control and flip over a bunch of times and that's the last I seen em."

Zella let out a wail. She bent to her waist, clasped her head, then slowly reached for Nehemiah's hand.

"If I hadn't been whoring, leaving him with his baby sister, none of it woulda happen. And so I have all this to think about ... all this ... shit. Then all of a sudden something happen when I kneel, something *good* come to mind, when I think 'bout what I done for them. Something I'd forgot a long time ago. And Seelos put it there, coming from the Father. And I'm standing there squeezing that fucka half to death. Got my arm round that statue ..." She stopped, breathing hard, then the words caught in her throat. "He'll give it to you too, sugar, you give him half a chance. *Come on, Delfeayo ...*"

Zella let go of Nehemiah and all she could see was him. She stepped forward in a trance, mesmerized by her own words. "He give me strength, baby boy, that's what I'm trying to tell you. Now you see? *You gotta try!*" She looked passionately at Delfeayo and, for a moment, seemed revived, unaware of anything on earth but her own longing to convince. She's in her own world, Annie thought, charismatic to the end, as though everything in her heart was exposed on stage and nobody in the audience can take their eyes off her.

Zella moved toward Feayo. "Nobody's alone." Her eyes begging him. "You jus ask, baby boy, and Seelos, he deliver." Voice light, rejoicing. "He'll protect you like he was guarding the fucking Wells Fargo full of cash. You gotta ask. *You gotta get down on your knees and ask!*"

Zella got down on her knees and tears fell from her eyes. There was no response from the corner and though the darkness had receded as the rain ceased outside, sudden light peering through the boarded window, Annie saw the dead-faced Feayo, mordantly still, turn away.

Zella's voice cracked: "What's the matter, baby boy? You ain't got no hope?"

There was silence inside the room as well as in the field and Annie felt the wonder of Zella's yearning as she waited, actually waited, for some response from him. He did not disappoint: "Ain't none of that done my daddy no good."

"Your daddy never done *hisself* no good. Let me tell you 'bout your daddy." Voice blasting, Zella got up. "You been hating that fucka 'cause he kill your daddy? I got news for you, son: Your daddy kill hisself."

She went on: "You think some demon took over? You think a thought walked out your head and led you 'cross that street and grabbed your hand and took that match and set the fire? That you didn't have no part in *this*? And now you planning to use that gun 'cause you stuck in a jam? *I may have raised fools but not one of em's a coward.* You did what you did 'cause you got hate in your heart. *Do something 'bout it. Ask Seelos for his help.*"

At that moment, Nehemiah took several steps forward so that he was in front of his Grandma. With back turned to Feayo, Nehemiah pressed his hands against Zella's waist in the gentlest manner, but with an intent that was clear he was gesturing her to the door, guiding her with grace, at the same time filling the room with calm and Annie, hope. Annie knew he was the only intervention that could bring forth good. She saw Zella, wide-eyed, staring, perhaps sensing this as well, staring at him in awe, as if remembering him for the first time, and then recognizing something beyond the boy had brought him forward. While it was written on her face the first instinct to resist, that knowledge seemed to make her hesitate, and then she yielded with an effort that sent a shudder down her body followed by profound acceptance, and, ultimately, relief. Zella, as if aware of where she'd almost gone, how dangerously close she came, turned and walked to the door and, soon after, Annie followed. When Zella was outside and Annie by the door, Annie turned and peeked in and she saw Nehemiah walk forward and stand to face Feayo.

Annie turned away, hearing murmurs at first, rather than words, sounds and intonations that made their way into vocabulary through their utterances, not vocabulary in the usual sense, but communication that transmitted a sense of familiarity and kindness, two cousins come together, alone again at last, gratefully alone, with a heartfelt outpouring that seeped outside the door where Annie huddled with Zella, as hallowed and longed for as sounds could describe. Nehemiah was speaking to him, and Annie could not hear clearly, and neither did she dare crack the door, for fear she would disturb the sound she could not create herself. For the first time Annie could remember, she felt herself relax. She looked and saw before her a cleansing of the sky and felt grateful, deeply relieved by the fresh and cleansing smell, craving what she saw: a new light out, the high branches of a giant oak moving through light in circular dances against the white sky, the breeze so cool she would like to take a nap in it, a nap that would last forever, the sounds coming from across the flooded street — sounds of water gushing from a drain — and she could see the furls of water on the sidewalk, falling like shallow waterfalls to the street. It was so mild and gentle and loving outside, it took her breath away. And then she heard a blast of gunfire and someone's shocked scream.

She sits in the foggy dark as if I'm no longer here, except for my spirit escaped from my body, or some ghost of a memory of friendship she can't forget, as if she has no other place to go but this forlorn and strangled room. If I could guide her to the door and tell her where, I'd hold on with every ounce of strength and get my feet behaving, or else I'd let her drag me out of here, having no goal in sight but smell of sky and looming twilight.

She's too sad to know my presence, longing for forgetfulness. Yet, she repeats what she cannot bear, trying to make sense of what she cannot know. She thinks I don't hear. Thinks I don't see. She thinks my mind is gone; I see and hear nothing. That my brain is full of nothing. I don't disagree with her on that. But I know she suffers as much as I. And that I can't bear the dark without her. There is somewhere I must go. She can get me out of here. There is something to be done. A living part to find. Under the bed — don't ask me why. We will find it if she takes me there.

If I get my feet behaving, I'll climb right out of here. There's just one small thing. It is beyond my ability to right. Sometimes I don't see my feet. Sometimes they disappear. Can never see the right side of me. Can't even feed myself. If she were to ask me who I am, I wouldn't know what to say. There would be a problem taking her anywhere. The door, I've forgotten that. Once, the doctor tried to shake my hand. I didn't know where my hand was. There's no more left of me. What's left is under the bed.

Memories spill from my brain like water from a table, sliding off the edge and vanishing out of sight. I don't know what left or right is. Or how to hold a pen. I can't even read. Not even a sign above the door. If I were to strain to see a single letter, I can barely remember that. "Have hope," somebody said. "Be happy for what you have." What I have is her. At night, she talks to me. Brings words into my head, stirring up memories. Causing me to think, lighting pictures in my head.

And then I remember the night. Remember the street. The street was my home once. Don't ask how long ago. The lights of the lamps wink through the trees. The breeze on my cheek like lights through Christmas trees. A rainbow above an ice cream shop. A whirring fan above a balcony. And next to it, on another balcony, feet cling to wrought iron, whiling away the night looking down upon the street. A thousand diamonds of shattered glass. The breeze on an evening sidewalk. I am clothed in loneliness, have been all my life, on a street of moving cars and shadowy sidewalks and broken glass — I remember that.

Then all my memories fade.

If I could remember who she is. She grieves as though her heart will break. The tree out on the street, it flashes green then red. Why do I remember that and remember nothing else? How the tar from the lamppost melts on the street on hot summer evenings when loneliness is as constant as street lights blinking on and off, where trees flash green and red? And here this woman sits. I do not know her name. I know I can't live without her. I cannot live without her.

X. till the fat lady sings

"Miz Annie, why you on the floor?"

"There's something under the cot."

"What?"

"I don't know."

"Then why you looking for it?"

"Leo told me it was here."

"Leo speaks to you?"

"No. Not really. Once he said, 'bed ... under bed ...' Then hours later, he said it again. So I looked under his bed at Charity and there was nothing. And the next day he repeated it, 'bed ... under bed ...' as if it was something that meant a lot to him. So I thought it must be here. This cot. Under this cot. Here in this back room."

"Get up. I'll find it for you."

"Nehemiah, thank you, honey."

Nehemiah got on his knees in the back room of the bookshop and pulled up the thin spread and looked under the cot and pulled out a duffle bag. It was green, caved in, and dusty. He unzipped it, took out a stack of papers. Annie knelt beside him, took the stack of papers from his hands, and straightened out the pages so that they were neat and organized. On each page, perhaps three hundred or more, and on both sides was someone's penciled writing. Annie glanced at the first page. Her hand trembled as she turned to the next. When she turned to the third page, she took her time to read. Her lips moved feverishly as she turned the page over and read, and then turned eagerly to the next page. She could hear Nehemiah's restless pacing, moving noisily about the room as if hoping she'd stop and notice him. Still, Annie could not keep her eyes off the page, desperate to read on, till she heard him halt in the middle of the room and come over to where she huddled.

"What's that you got?" he said, standing over Annie.

"A manuscript." She cleared her throat. "It's the draft of a novel."

"Leo's?"

"Leo's."

Annie turned back to the sheets of paper, turning a page, reading both sides of the next, placing the read page on the floor, perusing the next and the one after that, almost giddy to follow its path, overwhelmed with desire to savor what was before her till, suddenly, realizing her obligation, she hesitated and looked up. Nehemiah got down on the floor beside her, giving her permission, so it seemed, by his half-smile to let her do what she wanted, which was to read on. And this is what she did. He watched — she could feel his eyes on her — and abruptly she laughed. She turned so quickly he jumped. She put down the sheets of paper.

"Son of a bitch ..." she whispered.

She squeezed him.

"I knew it," she rejoiced.

"Knew what?"

"Leo, baby."

She picked up the papers, showed him the words centered on the first page, "Faulkner & Friends." She turned to the next page. "For Annie," it read. The third was filled with Leo's distinctive scrawl and in the upper right-hand corner in tiny letters was a name.

He looked at it. "Who's Marvin Everillo?"

"Leo."

"Leo wrote this" — Nehemiah gestured to the page — "and put somebody else's name on it?"

Annie's eyes wandered to the kitchen table. Here in the back room, nearly half their things were packed in preparation for the move. Father Rigoli, hearing about the tragedy, that Zella died of a heart attack after her grandson shot himself and that Annie and Nehemiah, evicted, had to be out as soon as possible, had agreed to let the two of them move into the tiny space above the gift shop as planned, even without Zella Theophile — in honor of Zella Theophile — which was the least he could do after all Zella had done for the Francis Seelos shrine.

And so half their things were packed. The kitchen table, at the center of their activities, was bare, giving the room an effluvium of sorrow and loss. Annie remembered kneading dough at that table to make spinach pies to serve to the very first discussion group and how she'd fretted, fearing Leo might not show up. But not really. To be perfectly honest, she never had the slightest doubt. She knew the character of the man, though she hadn't known him for very long. Knew in her heart the kind of man he was, someone who would never go back on his word. Knew also that the group would be guided by a genius. How did she know? The man who wrote *Second-Story Window* could be no less.

When he first told her he was Marvin Everillo, the news came as a shock. It was like a precious stone, a rare diamond slipped onto her finger, the presence of the man. And like a master's work of art, merely being in the same room with him shone a light upon her existence.

She never saw him write but once. He never wrote in the shop. She saw him trudge off one morning after having his chicory coffee, mumbling he was going to catch a streetcar. He carried a stack of loose leaf papers and she asked where he was going. Latter Library, he told her. Later that day, she'd been driving in that direction, Uptown on St. Charles Avenue, to deliver books to a customer and thought she'd offer him a ride home. She made her way up the creaky stairs of the Latter, saw him sitting at a round table on the second floor alone and, amid the clamor of school children and chattering Uptown matrons, saw what he was doing. He put down his pencil when he saw her at the head of the stairs. When she saw the way he looked at her, she regretted intruding upon his privacy.

He was a private man, filled with secrecies. He was a man of pride as well, and he never slept in the shop. Oh, once when he'd been sick. And there were times when he'd take a shower in the back before leading a discussion. Or stay late reading to Nehemiah. But as often as she and Zella would insist, he never accepted their offers to stay the night. She never asked where he did sleep, never pretended she didn't know. And he never brought it up.

But she knew. One night shortly before midnight less than a week following the grand opening, she'd chanced to walk to the all-night Swifty Serve several blocks down the street to get milk for her morning cereal when she saw him lying in an alley between two buildings, a thin blanket over him. At first, she thought it some homeless bum, not an unfamiliar sight in the Irish Channel, but then to her astonishment she recognized something familiar — the mustache — and the dark beard streaked with silver and something about the facial profile. Peering from beneath the blanket was a portion of beard and the familiar cheekbone and the eye, in profile, closed and in shadow, where she could barely make out who he was beneath a light shining on him from the side of a building.

It shocked her. There was a great disparity between the essence — spirit — of the great writer she adored and the pitiful wretch beneath the blanket. How amazing it hadn't taken her long to forget about the frayed clothing after first meeting him and even forget he was Marvin Everillo and become aware of the soul, or was it the character — the dignity, intelligence, and proud demeanor — of the man and, in later conversations, the compassion most assuredly born of hardship. She was the kind of person who never paid attention to outward appearances, always focusing on inner qualities, so that once knowing the person's essence it was easy to forget the rest: the skin color and quality of garment.

But that night, shortly before midnight, she saw what others saw. Maybe she had put this man Everillo on a pedestal because she wanted to believe that an angel had deposited him on her doorstep to make her know that in the midst of the rot and decay of life something glorious could happen. She wanted to believe he had come into her life to encourage and inspire and fill her once again with hope, the hope she'd had as a child, that life could be beautiful and radiant and that nothing could go wrong.

But there he was, sleeping in a space no bigger than six by four, an alleyway between two buildings, the rest of it concealed behind a gate. Within this space, he had spread a sheet on the cold hard pavement, the thin cotton blanket drawn slightly above his chin. Perhaps it was the cheerful colors of the shotgun double or respectability of the gallery that made him feel safe in this cold alleyway, a specious and traitorous perception, a cruel betrayal of faith, and she feared for his life. A smack on the head with a beer bottle by some sadistic thug, a knifing by some maniac, could put an end to his suffering. And maybe that would be a blessing. But not for her.

She had kneeled beside him, squinting, straining to see if his eyes might be partly open so that he might be half awake and she could rouse him to conversation. She knew she must do something, must not let him sleep on this cold hard ground with the mercury hovering at 25°. Nothing about him deserved this kind of life. If she could wake him, she would invite him to sleep in her shop where he'd be safe and protected by those who loved him. *Now where had that come from?* By those who *cared*. There, that was better. But she knew the man, knew him as well as anyone could in so short a span of time, knew he would be humiliated by her seeing him this way.

So she waited.

He came the next day. Nearly every day he came, had a habit of dropping in (as she knew he would; book addicts like him can't stay away from books too long), never overstaying his welcome, ensconced in the armchair for several hours at a stretch, accepting a cup of joe, chatting up her and Zella. Zella liked to tease, she could be downright merciless, but it only enlivened him. He'd even endeared himself to Nehemiah; the boy was drawn to him.

Sometimes when she entered the front room, she'd see him read to Nehemiah or recite a child's tale she wouldn't think a grown man would know by heart. And it gave her pleasure having him visit. He was honest and true, a false word never leaving his lips, a rare and precious quality, his genuineness and honesty, his down-to-the-core reverence for truth.

He was most that way when talking about books. You could never get away with belittling an author he esteemed or dismissing a book he respected. Once she'd called Jean Stafford a drunk. "She may have been a drunk," he fired back, "but she was the greatest short story writer of her generation." He'd read her novels and all of her stories and his favorite story was, "I Love Someone." (He revealed to her his sentimental favorites: John Cheever's "The Death of Justina," Faulkner's "A Rose for Emily," Scott Fitzgerald's "Babylon Revisited," Willa Cather's "Neighbour Rosicky," Lawrence Sargeant Hall's "The Ledge," Saul Bellow's "Seize the Day," James Joyce's "The Dead.")

Another time, she appeared to trivialize Walker Percy by saying he tried to persuade his reader that the Catholic view of the human condition was the only one that made sense. Pausing to consider that, vertical lines fanning out across his brow, he said irritably, "Yes, of course, that may be true. But no one had his *integrity*." He cited Percy's favorite saying: nothing is worse than a novel that seeks to edify the reader.

Most of all, he admired writers who stood up for their beliefs. He cited Katherine Ann Porter's mania for not letting an editor touch one word of her work and for staying true to her art despite many years of living in poverty. From the way he spoke, it was obvious his best friends were writers. He liked them dead. Nobody else came close. There seemed to be no writer he hadn't read: Forster, Mauriac, Simenon, Celine, Waugh, Burroughs, Moravia, Perelman. And there were few esoteric facts he didn't know. He knew H.G. Wells was Nabokov's favorite writer when he was a boy and that he had once described Joyce's *Finnegans Wake* as a "cancerous growth of fancy word-tissue." He knew Isak Dinesen was really the Danish Baroness Karen Christentze Blixen-Finecke. He knew Richard Wright was born in 1908 and Eudora Welty one year later and that they lived eighteen blocks away from each other in Jackson, Mississippi. With his knowledge and love of books and writers, she couldn't help wondering what he'd be like leading a discussion group. And she couldn't wait for the day he'd let that intelligence and passion loose.

Next morning after seeing him in the alley, she made him an offer. "Hey," she called out after he walked into the shop. It was ten o'clock, an hour after she'd opened. "If you'll be the moderator on a regular basis, you can crash here every night."

His eyes clouded. "I have a place to sleep," he said stiffly. He approached a shelf, picked out a book. "But thank you anyway."

"I'm sure you do," she said lightly. "But not everyone gets such magnificent company as Zella and me to crash with. You can sleep here on the sofa. The boys'll sleep on the floor. And Zella and I'll sleep in the cot in back. It'll be your payback for leading the group."

"That's nice," he said abruptly. "I intend to do it only once."

"Well then, you can sleep here anyway," she insisted. "We'll have ourselves a slumber party. I'll fix popcorn, we'll tell stories. And when the weather gets warmer, you can go back to your regular place."

He'd taken Gabriel García Márquez's *One Hundred Years of Solitude* off the shelf and was ensconced in his favorite chair. She teased him, saying she thought he only read dead writers. He gazed at the floor, lips drawn, not really focusing on anything, seeming preoccupied and irritable. His hand shook as it rested on the cover; he looked thinner than usual, sickly, the yellow tinge to his skin alarming. He got up, returned the book to the shelf, and wordlessly walked out.

She hadn't seen him since that day and worried more about his welfare than she did about his not showing up. He was proud, certainly, and sensitive, so instinctive and sharp he probably sensed she'd seen him sleeping on the street and feeling ashamed, not wanting to be the object of pity, probably just didn't want to see her for awhile. She had not worried about his not appearing. He was not the type to renege on a commitment or violate her trust; she knew enough about him or believed she did. Believed he was not the dishonorable type.

And so, the morning of the book discussion, she made sure the chairs were stacked in an orderly fashion, in a semi-circle facing the moderator's chair, and that there would be enough on hand in case the event magically drew a crowd. She went to the back room, peeked inside the tiny fridge at the cream cheese balls on platters and Lebanese spinach pies she'd baked that morning and the sausage bread squares. (She loved to cook and had gone all out for this special occasion.) And then she checked to see if she had enough wine and apple-cranberry cider and coffee and plastic glasses and Styrofoam cups. She poured a bit more water into the vase, poured herself two shots of bourbon, and sat down and waited.

He came. He did his best. And that was all she could ever ask. But she never saw him write. In all the time she'd known him, which, she admitted, hadn't been for very long, she'd never seen him place the green duffle bag under the cot. She'd never even seen him *with* the bag. Mostly, when he came and went, she never noticed what was in his hand. But then, she never paid attention to his comings and goings, wasn't the observant type, being busy with other things.

So it must not have been that long ago, after he'd finished writing his novel, on a day he'd slipped in and she'd been distracted, that he'd left it on one of his visits. It would always be a mystery. But that was the logical place for it, of course — not in a garbage bag on the street where it'd get wet or lost or stolen. She had a suspicion his novel meant more to him than life. Why else would he sleep in the street and hide the manuscript under the cot?

Nehemiah frowned.

"No," she said. "Leo didn't put somebody else's name on it. Honey, Marvin *is* his name."

"Then why did he lie to us?"

"He told me his real name the first day we met. But he made me promise not to tell. He wanted everybody to call him Leo."

"Why?"

Annie thought about it and had no answer. It was at that moment she noticed something as Nehemiah waited for a response. His skin was sallow. He was thin, a thinness she hadn't noticed during the procession of sad days suddenly instilling fear in her. Once, she'd been responsible only for herself; now she was in charge of all the treasures on earth: Nehemiah, Leo, and now this stack of papers. She made a promise to herself to take Nehemiah for a checkup.

She remained silent, trying to figure it out. Impatiently, he made his way to the door. He stood looking into the front room. She watched. There was a weakness in the way he moved, a frailty that worried her. The deterioration was visible. She wondered if he might be sick. She herself had been feeling strange. There were periods in her day when she'd become anxious and restless. Sometimes it was impossible to get the work done, to concentrate. As determined as she was to work, she couldn't seem to light on anything. She'd always been a hard worker but during those strange, unsettling periods she couldn't seem to focus. She blamed it on recent events. The horrors that had come down on them had been a terrible shock to her system, but she assumed she'd get over it, be her old self again in time.

Looking now at Nehemiah, she saw a gaunt child in a dirty shirt, frayed pants, and socks with holes in them. He hadn't had enough to eat and his hair needed cutting. So obsessed with her own suffering, she hadn't noticed the last time he'd showered or what he'd had for supper when she was away at the hospital.

He stood limp, feet apart. She longed to go over and put her arms around him, then remembered Feayo and the last moments they'd shared together and turned away from him in horror. She got up, opened the fridge, threw away an opened can of root beer and chunk of moldy cheese.

"Know what?" she said, turning.

He didn't bother to look her way.

"Whatever reason he had for not wanting anyone to know had nothing to do with us."

She came to him, took his hand. She led him to the table. They sat down together. His cheeks were drawn, a green cast to his skin, mostly from loneliness, she figured, than anything else, a devastation of grief and deep isolation.

"You see" — she measured her words — "he wanted to be known as Leo, even for me to call him Leo. And that's the way we will honor him. He was ... *private*. The kind of private we'll never understand because we're not him. He needed for nobody in the world to know anything about him."

Nehemiah seemed to take that in and, when a car honked outside, shattering the silence, she was aware of his thin words: "But he and I was friends."

She thought of a high school buddy she hadn't seen in years. An invisible shield between him and everybody. He had a mama whom he adored, who'd died when he was young, just like Nehemiah. As a grownup he'd appear at parties by himself, staying an hour and then disappearing, the joke of everyone who branded him the mystery man, never staying long enough to get to know anybody. She saw him once in the Quarter, staggering, passing her by without recognition, bug-eyed and in a blackout.

How brave. Nehemiah precocious, always wanting to know; Leo eager to give forth his knowledge. Nehemiah loved to be read to, Leo gloried in it. Leo could read a soup can in a trash bin with eloquence and passion.

"My guess," she mused, "was that he felt everything he ever wrote after *Second-Story Window* would never measure up. Did you know he almost won the Pulitzer Prize? You know what that is? The best damn writing prize in the whole wide world."

She looked at him, glowing. "I guess he hid his real name because he wanted some privacy to write his next book. He had to write from a place that was only his, some very, very private place. And that book had to have a different author to be accepted by the public. Sure, his name was on the draft you saw. But my hunch is that once the manuscript was completely finished, he'd try to have it published under the name Leo for protection against critics who love to crucify an author after a first book achieves success. I am ... I don't know ... it's a theory ... I'm only guessing ..."

She turned in shame from her useless babbling.

She thought she heard him gasp.

"But why he lie to *me*?"

"Because ..." she stammered, "... he wanted ... *protection* ... or ... a new life. You know he went to prison. Maybe he got tired of himself and wanted to be someone else. I don't know. I don't *know* ... I have no idea. What does it matter? He loved us, can't you tell?"

She stood up and walked away. She glanced into the front room to what used to be the bookshop. Boxes were all over the floor, half filled with books. They should have been out at least a month ago but what was Mr. Zibilich going to do, kick them into the street? She turned. "He spent almost every waking hour with us when he wasn't off writing. And most of that with you. We were his *family*, Nehemiah. So what does it matter if he didn't give you his real name?"

She waited for him to say something.

Slowly, he looked up. "Maybe when he gets better you think he could tell me?"

She entered the front room and sat in Leo's chair. She looked out the window. The sidewalk was empty in front of the shop. Not a single car passed. Suddenly, in the half light, she felt herself return to a far different time, becoming what she'd been before laying eyes upon this neighborhood. Frantically, she got up and rummaged through one of the boxes and, finding what she wanted, brought it to him. "Here," she said, placing it in his hands. "From now on, you and I, we're going to read this everyday."

Tenderly, she took it from him and slowly lifted it. "Because this is going to tell us everything we want to know. And you'll have to be satisfied because Leo can't tell us."

"This the book he wrote?"

"Yes."

"The one that nearly won the prize?"

"That's right."

"Will you read me some?"

She turned to her favorite scene:

*

Before dawn, he went to her rooming house. The sky was blue velvet. Across the street stood the Church of the Blessed Sacrament. A cat lay on the front step. In the foyer of a rectory adjoining the church, a light was on. He got out of the car, walked up five steps and sat in a vinyl chair on the porch of the rooming house. The building was a wooden structure badly in need of repair. On a second-floor gallery, a railing leaned far out so that if one rested his weight on it he'd plunge through the rotting wood onto a banana tree below. A single lantern illuminated the porch. Six feet from where he sat, a rope swing hung. He'd sit and wait for her.

Of all the times he'd dropped her off, he hadn't noticed whether she entered through the front or around the side to get to her room. He peeked and saw there was no door around the side so he knew she must enter through the front. He tried the door. It was locked. He hated to knock and wake her landlord, so he sat back in the chair. The sky was turning light. A drizzle had begun. Across the street, an old nun entered the church. Far off, birds chattered and he was reminded of wild parakeets that perched atop palm trees overlooking Biscayne Bay in Miami where he once visited. There were banana trees in the front yard, their green fruit clustered near the top. Across the street, in a house next to the rectory, a pale glow of light illuminated rose curtains in a second-story window. Mosquitoes knapped at his ankles. He couldn't stand to wait any longer. He got up and left the porch and went to the front yard and yelled, "Di," to an upstairs window. "Di …" he yelled again, "Di, Di, Di, Di, Di …" Still, no answer. He knocked on the door. An old woman appeared.

*

She closed the book. The details weren't quite as she remembered but the scene was still beautiful to her as was the memory of what came next. She wondered what Nehemiah thought. He was quiet, looking distracted, his eyes fixed on the book.

"And Leo ..." he pondered, "he can't tell us why he change his name?"

"You know he got shot."

"And what that done?"

She shoved the book aside. "This is what the doctor said: the bullet lodged in the posterior parieto-occipital regions of the brain and destroyed the tissue there. He's suffering from progressive, irreversible atrophy of that part of the brain." She nodded toward the book. "We're going to start from the beginning then read a little everyday. And when we finish, we're going to start on that stack of papers. And then you'll know Leo better than he knows himself."

"Can't I see him?"

"No, not right now. But we'll take him home someday. He'll live with us."

"He'll be able to talk?"

"Not like before."

"He'll remember me?"

"It's hard to say."

"He'll be able to read?"

"I don't think that's in the cards."

"He'll be able to walk? He won't be able to write? He won't ... remember me?"

"Nehemiah, right now, he can't orient himself in space. He doesn't know left from right. He has no memory. You and I, we don't know what he's capable of. There's scar tissue that produced the atrophy that's only going to get worse."

"What's atrophy?"

"Wasting away. It's like something wasting away."

"He'll never get better?"

"That's not for us to say. And we can never let him think that. He knows he's failing in every way as a human being. And he ... *suffers* from it. He's lost everything. He can hardly say words to express himself. He can't write. He can't pick up a fork. He doesn't even know what a fork is. He can't control a pencil. Add or subtract. And yet the one thing he has left is the understanding of how much he's lost. The one part of the brain that wasn't harmed in any way was the part that allows him to know how bad it really is and desperately want to get better. That's what torments him. We can't take away his hope. It's the only thing he has to live for."

"I can read to him?"

"Sure ..."

"I'll teach him how to write."

"So you're going to be the teacher now, huh, Nehemiah?" She got up and found herself staring into the front room, as if the room held an answer. "I wish there was some way we could keep this place," she mumbled. "It would be just you and me and Leo." She sat down and thought about it and then she turned to him. "His life may not be over. And neither is ours. You know it's not over till the fat lady sings. And maybe someday — if you do a good enough job — Leo will explain to you what that means."

XI. in the dryer, tumbling

Nehemiah sat in the back seat, Miz Annie driving and Leo beside her. Nehemiah gazed at the Avenue with all its trees and old houses. On the way over Miz Annie saw things, asked Leo to repeat them, things like Creole cottage and wandering jew and cypress doors and elephant ears. Sometimes Leo looked weird, like he'd been kidnapped by a bunch of crazies, but Miz Annie was only following orders, doing what the doctor told her. Nehemiah helped Leo out of the car. They sat by the water's edge.

June 6th — his birthday.

The only thing he and Miz Annie asked was that he learn one new word. But Nehemiah knew it wasn't going to be easy, knew what they were up against. Leo not only had no memory, he couldn't see things on the right side. The right side of whatever he looked at didn't even exist. It'd be like holding up two hands and seeing only the left. And not only that, Miz Annie told him, Leo saw things that weren't there. The scar tissue did that. She said it stimulated nerve cells that made Leo see things, like his head was too big for his body and his body was all shrunk up, that's the way he saw himself.

Leo put his hand in the water. He stared at it real hard. There were ripples crossing over, a million runners in white. Nehemiah thought that real cool, that and the blue sky and squirrels running on phone lines and couples strolling with their dogs, babies riding on the backs of bikes, pelicans in the bayou. It was all he could ever ask for on this beautiful spring morning. But veins popped out of Leo's neck and his eyes got as big as saucers, so Nehemiah reached to take his hand.

"Bayou St. John, Leo," he said, teaching him some new words.

It was his job to repeat things to bring Leo's memory back so one day he'd talk in sentences and maybe even write. But he couldn't imagine living like that, being nothing but a baby. And at that moment he was freaking out, shoulders shaking, Miz Annie comforting him, trying to calm poor Leo down. There was only one thing Nehemiah knew: they had their work cut out for them 'cause Leo didn't know nothing. Everything he'd ever learn, he and Miz Annie would have to teach him.

Miz Annie sliced a piece of chocolate pudding cake she got at the Winn-Dixie.

"Cake ... cake ..." she said to Leo.

"Cake ... cake ..." he repeated.

It was like filling up an ocean something sucked out overnight. But that was cool. It'd be all right. They had time, they'd work it out. Nehemiah just got out of school for the summer and Miz Annie no longer worked. She and he were living free up in the rooms above the gift shop. They were broke but weren't starving; Father Rigoli fed them sometimes. And they'd make it till they got on their feet again. They were putting everything they had, all their energy and time, into Leo and his brain, feeding up memories so he could write again someday. Working like they believed in miracles, that's what Grandma'd say. And at the same time, working on a plan to get Leo's book published.

Miz Annie typed up the pages. It was called *Faulkner & Friends*. Miz Annie said she'd write the editors of the publishing house of his first book, tell em what he'd done, get em up to snuff. They thought Leo'd died or something after he got out of prison — died or disappeared. Just like Leo, cover up his tracks. And Miz Annie said she'd put the pages in a box and send them off. And their eyes would pop out after they'd see the stuff he wrote.

"It's about us," Miz Annie told him. "And if you think it's only about a bookshop, you've got a big surprise coming. It's brilliant ..." she gushed, "the language

something you don't read today. We're living with a *genius*
…"

She said that all the time.

Nehemiah took turns reading with her. Miz Annie'd read a chapter one day, he'd read a chapter the next day. One night, Nehemiah was dying to know how the book finally ended 'cause the book was really long. He'd pleaded with her to tell him but she was tight-lipped about it. She herself knew how it ended, she'd spent the whole night reading. So Nehemiah kept on begging.

"Can't you give me a hint?"

"A big part of the plot," she said, "is about a boy based on you, only he's older than you. He's nineteen. He comes into the shop and we have a novel writing competition and the boy's the big winner. And not only that, he wins a New York publishing contract and the book he writes gets published and they make a movie out of it. So the boy gets rich and famous."

"How a boy that young gone write a book that good?"

"Have you ever heard of Truman Capote? At nineteen, he won the O. Henry award for a short story," she told him. "The great writer William Styron called him a master of the language before he was even old enough to vote."

Miz Annie said that another writer was seventeen when he got his first story published. "And, later, he wrote more than fifty plays, a book of poetry, four collections of stories, two novels." His name was Tennessee.

"Age doesn't mean a thing," she said, "when you're born with a rare talent."

Then she told him part of the plot: That these characters who hung out at the shop, all these folks who helped the boy who was alone and poor and friendless and who worked with him on the book, they got together with the boy to build a huge recreation center in the bombed-out

Central City where all the killings were going on. And there was a swimming pool there and a big basketball court and tutors and mentors and musicians to teach jazz and writers to teach fiction and folks to teach shipbuilding and lots of other things at that center so that kids with no skills didn't have to hang out in the streets. And the government played no part in it, it was run by a foundation, and all because of a bookshop named *Faulkner & Friends*.

"Only, Nehemiah," — she leaned in — "I'm not telling you how it ends. That's for you to find out. For you to read to me and me to read to you, one chapter at a time."

All she ever wanted was to get Leo's book published.

"What if they don't want it?" he asked.

"*Of course,* they'll want it," she scolded. "They're not crazy, after all. Who wouldn't want to publish the work of Marvin Everillo?"

Only, she swore she wouldn't betray him by getting it published under his real name. She didn't think he'd like that. She'll make them publish it under the name Leo, the assumed name of the secret writer, the 'pen name,' she called it, and they'll go along with that, it'll be a great publicity stunt.

"The public will go nuts trying to figure out who wrote it, put Leo on the bestseller list. Not that he needs trickery or gimmickry, his work stands on its own."

She had it all covered, let Leo have his privacy. Miz Annie was cool that way. Then they'd make a million bucks — she, Leo, and Nehemiah — and get themselves a house. All three living together, two writers and a bookstore owner, 'cause Nehemiah was going to be a writer too.

Then Miz Annie would open shop. She was nothing if not obsessed about it. Even after all she went through. She wanted to own a bookshop. She wanted it on Magazine Street. But this time she'd buy the place. And nobody'd have to buy a book. Just come over and read, don't worry if you can't afford it. She wanted everyone to feel at home.

"We'll make enough money from our published books." She smiled. "*You* too, Nehemiah. You'll be the best writer of them all. You're a great talent, my little man. And the material, with all you've been through, you'll have enough to fill a thousand books."

Living on hope.

First things first. They had a million things to do, keep them occupied.

First thing: new word. The doctor said one new word a day. Like an apple a day. She threw a million his way. His brain was going to explode if she didn't let it rest awhile. She patted Leo on the shoulder.

"Be careful, don't fall in the water." Then, "Water … water …" She stood up. "Let's go take a walk."

She held Leo under one arm and Nehemiah held him under the other and they climbed up the slope till they reached Moss Street then crossed Moss Street and headed for the cemetery.

As they walked up Esplanade Avenue, Leo stared at a streak of white from a jet plane in the sky, fascinated as a baby. White crosses peeked above a brick side wall straight ahead and there was a statue with wings and then Leo jumped, real jittery, when he saw a squirrel cross his path; then they entered the main gate. There, in front of them, breaking the boredom of all that white going back at least a mile stood a bright-gold priest statue towering over fake flowers.

"Padre Pio," Miz Annie said, excited, grateful for a new word.

She went on to read the plaque, something about how this humble Capuchin Friar surprised the world with his life of prayer and how his body, marked by a stigmata, showed the connection between death and resurrection.

"What's a stigmata?" Nehemiah asked.

"It's marks like a crucifixion wound."

Then she repeated, "stigmata ... stigmata," teaching Leo a new word, not thinking all these fancy words were going to fry poor Leo's brain. Leo stared into the friar's eyes and he seemed scared half to death because the eyes stared right back at him, deep and hard and close. Miz Annie moved on, repeating, "urn ... urn," pointing to one as tall as Nehemiah, with pink and white paper flowers. Iron chairs stood in front of a tomb as big as a small house with a life-sized angel on it and that's where they stopped to rest, Miz Annie sitting next to Leo, taking his hand and holding it, all the while looking across the Avenue. She kept staring past the friar to a house with a lot of stairs and seemed peaceful and satisfied, almost like she was happy. Smiling like she really meant it. She stood up and walked on.

They passed another statue. It was a face Nehemiah recognized: the face of Mother Teresa, hands bent in prayer, holding her rosary, and at the base of the statue, it read, "If you pray, you will have faith. If you have faith, you will love ..." and something else below it but he couldn't read it for the tall grass. They headed out through another gate and on to a coffee house.

They were at the Fair Grinds Coffeehouse, not far from the race track. Leo looked up from his chair to see a picture on the wall of three horses racing toward a finish line, two of them in the lead, the other a length behind. Leo's eyes devoured the picture then he sank, limp, looking lost, and it dawned on Nehemiah, *he can't remember.* It was all as confusing to him as if he were in a dryer tumbling with the wet clothes, staring at computers on tables, hearing music from wall speakers, seeing the moon, stars and fish painted on the chairs (thank god, Miz Annie was at the counter else she'd be teaching him a new word) — all meaning everything and nothing to him. And it dawned on Nehemiah it'd take a million years to bring Leo to himself and that they were never going to do it. He was never going to learn. He'd lost way too much.

But it was cool. It'd be all right.

They were all here together, which is more than a lot of people have. And since it was Leo's birthday, they had one more place to go.

They walked past the Zoom Szalon and La Boulangerie Bakery, Miz Annie saying those bullshit words, and Leo trudging along, taking it all in, both of them holding onto him, since he couldn't see anything on the right and might bump into a wall or something. Miz Annie climbed into the driver's seat but she didn't make a move to start the engine. She sat silent, awestruck, mouth opened, eyes glazed, staring at a blanket of branches high above the Avenue. She had the strangest, dumb look on her face. Nehemiah didn't know what was going on, like she was far-off or doped up or in some magical, mysterious trance. She sat that way a long time, totally forgetting them, so Nehemiah had to nudge her, "Miz Annie, let's get going."

It was her idea to go to Audubon Park to have a picnic to celebrate his birthday. Leo had turned 40. But she didn't go anywhere near the park. They were driving along Esplanade. They passed a park across from Whole Foods and another before they got to North Broad. Nehemiah guessed she might be thinking about parks 'cause, not too long after that, she was making a turn on North Rocheblave, and it was a one-way and Nehemiah kept yelling "Turn 'round!" 'fore she got the picture.

They were on Esplanade again. She was making a turn on North Tonti and she must have realized she was all confused and going the wrong way 'cause she saw Ursuline and turned there. Miz Annie was all messed up, her mind spinning like ceiling fan blades and, before long, they were in Tremé. Then they reached Marais Street, near the tall gates behind the Municipal Auditorium. And there, prowling the streets like a pack of wild dogs, some rough looking dudes standing in doorways. She was in Tremé again, trying to find her way out, and she wasn't listening to a word he said so he gave up and watched the scenery: the strays and boarded houses, the wide streets and little hotels and all those Baptist churches, and corner stores with signs over doors, saying *Papa Joe's spicy beans*, and another, about chicken wings, and Nehemiah saw a little sign on a fence in a church yard, *"Hot Fish Plates, only $5.00,"* and realized he was hungry. So they stopped there and got some plates. Then they passed by some narrow streets with bright painted cottages with gingerbread woodwork and little potted palms and, soon, they were facing North Rampart and Nehemiah was freaking out. *"Turn here, Miz Annie. Turn here ..."*

Miz Annie, she was looking like she'd never been so relieved in all her life 'cause it was pretty clear how to get to Audubon Park from North Rampart Street. When they finally got to where they were going and spread a sheet over the grass and took out the fish fries, Miz Annie didn't say a word. She didn't point out anything either, just sat looking at the lagoon, not confused like before, just tired, really tired. And there was something wrong with that. Definitely, Nehemiah knew. And after they made their way home, Miz Annie slept all afternoon.

Behind these dull eyes, he sees a hero's heart. He asks do I remember. I say, "No ... I don't know ..." Do you remember your name? Remember being shot? "No. I don't know ..." Remember where you were born? Who your mama was? Some ache of a memory slides through my confusion. But do I have the words? They are so far away. The only thing I know is that this dizziness won't stop. He shoves a book across the table. I pick it up and hold it. He lifts a thumb in the air and smiles.

Her eyes dim with sadness. I try to walk and she looks away. Something in me died. She knows, we all know. Always she reads to me. Trying to bring back something else. What it is will never come. I chase after it in my sleep. I gauge my progress by her eyes, sometimes shining, with light. And then one failed move; it is beyond what she can hide.

The boy has more of it. It is himself it rises from. If it were one small part me, I would keep that forever. I touch the voice in this close space and let it lift my willing body and coach this dreaming spirit to learn one new word.

My life has come to this: a day I have no capacity to know. Words on a page that are the keys to I know not what. A horror that will never end, a grief that will never die, the brain brilliant and perfect at last in its own doom.

XII. ice melting on sidewalk

"Miz Annie, whatcha got?"

She was picking up the boneless short rib, like she thought that was what they came for, one after another, tossing them in the cart, going for the pricey stuff, the twenty dollar size, like they ate that everyday.

"Maybe them chicken wings, huh, Miz Annie?"

But she wouldn't even take the hint. All they'd ever come for was the beans and rice.

"We ain't brought that much cash ..." Nehemiah didn't think she even heard. "You hear me, Miz Annie?"

Her hands never stopped moving, like they were pulled by some puppeteer with strings attached to her. She was smiling, like she was pleased, like picking books up from off a shelf — hey, wait, now Nehemiah got the deal.

"Hey, Miz Annie, how 'bout let's go? We only come here for the Blue Runner. We're having red beans tonight —" It was like talking to the funny pages.

"Hey, Miz Annie!"

Something was going on. It had started with the birthday ride down Esplanade three days ago. Then last night, she'd pulled out a suitcase and taken her clothes from out of the drawers. "You 'bout to go somewhere?" he'd asked. She wasn't wasting any time.

"Have to get the books," she cried, "Get going ..."

"Going where?"

"Get packed and out of here ..."

And then she gave Nehemiah a look like the bad times was chasing after her. She plopped down on the bed, stared ahead like her mind was blown. And there was Leo at the kitchen table giving her his full attention. And Nehemiah thought, *I'm the only one left got anything worth saving.*

Nehemiah sat down, put his arm around her shoulders. She was nothing but a little girl lost on the boulevard. If it hadn't been for her, they'd be nothing but blocks of ice tossed out on the pavement, melting when the sun came up.

"Hey, Miz Annie ..." — he took her hand — "you ain't going nowhere without me."

Her hands never stopped moving. A mountain of pork piled in that cart. Now she was going for the ground chuck, beef brisket, sirloin tip. The butcher behind the counter was giving her the evil eye. There was mumbling up and down the aisles. They were like a moving van for the hungry. Now everything was on the floor. She was doing something he couldn't believe. He'd never seen anything like it. She was taking off her shirt. Tossing it in the meat bin. Unzipping her skirt. *"Stop ... don't do that!"* Nehemiah saw something in her eyes. She was taking it all in, the guards, cart, looking down at the shirt he held. She was taking it away from him and sliding her arms into the sleeves, shaking so bad she couldn't button anything up. Nehemiah grabbed her arm. They had to get moving. Them suckers was bearing down on them.

XIII. confrontation in the park

"Emma Rose ..."

"Why, look who's here."

"It's nice to see you. How've you been?"

"I've been fine. How are you?"

"I've been better."

"Is that right?"

"Would you mind if I sat down?"

Annie stood over Emma Rose in the lush grass at Audubon Park. She watched the dumpy figure in white Bermudas shield her eyes against the glaring sun. Emma Rose Brewer, one finger touching an open page of a bonded leather hardback, suddenly slammed the book shut, a move motivated by anger, no doubt. But surely there were other emotions at play, among them curiosity, to know why she was here, what on earth had brought her here? Annie swayed. She didn't exactly collapse but made a less than graceful descent, placing hands strategically upon the grass to block her fall, steadying herself as she carefully got to her knees. Annie positioned herself on the grass, hands on either side of her, and stretched out her legs. She felt shaky, a bit afraid. She wondered if Emma Rose noticed.

"Are you all right?" Emma Rose asked.

"Haven't been myself lately."

"Have you been sick?"

"Yes, I have."

"Well ..." Emma Rose shrugged. "I'm sorry to hear that." But there was no sympathy in her voice. And then she fidgeted and half turned and, with a show of distaste and displeasure, acted as if she were getting up to leave. But then curiosity got the better of her. "With what?" she said, turning around.

"It's my ... behavior."

"Your what?"

"I've become ... repetitious." Annie took a handkerchief from her skirt pocket and wiped her face. She gazed at her outstretched legs and folded her arms in front of her. She was facing the lagoon. The jogging path was no farther than fifty feet away, the lagoon forty feet beyond that. Annie caught a glimpse of the brackish water, looked fixedly at it, momentarily forgetting Emma Rose. When next she turned back, the older woman, sitting on a linen sheet on the green grass beneath a giant oak tree, was glaring at her.

"Your face is pale," Emma Rose said curiously, "and there're dark shadows under your eyes."

"I'm heavier than when you last saw me."

"Well ..." said Emma Rose, "I'm not one to judge you for that. But what do you mean, 'repetitious'? I don't know what you mean by that."

"I keep repeating phrases," Annie mumbled, looking distractedly at the lagoon, "flushing the toilet too many times, stacking food in a cart till everything topples over. I wander from my room to this very same spot, over and over and over again ..." Her words trailed off. Mesmerized by the lagoon, her voice dropped to nearly a whisper. "I always see you here, Emma Rose. Always in this same place."

"Stalking me?"

A young girl tossed bread crumbs on the grass and into the lagoon, luring Annie's attention her way. On the jogging path, heading for the spot where the girl stood, seven children suddenly appeared, their voices thrilled and beckoning. A child with flaxen hair ran ahead of the others, stopped, waited, and when everyone reached the grass, including a woman with a singular braid down her back, they all gathered behind the girl with crumbs. Joggers grunted as they passed. Three men, wearing the football colors of Tulane University, talked familiarly with one another as they jogged. Ducks swam toward the bank. A squirrel perched on the thick root of a live oak moved toward the crumbs. "No," Annie murmured. "I wouldn't say that exactly. It has to do with what I've got."

Annie sat transfixed by the sights and sounds and smells of nature. And when she looked back at Emma Rose, it was clear the old woman was pondering her choices: Should she get up and walk away or continue her line of questioning or wait for some sign of what to do? And there was another choice: Call the cops.

"*Look here*," Emma Rose raised her voice. She twisted the wrapper of a half-empty bag of crackers, hastily putting it inside its box. "I believe your name is Ms. Ajami, isn't it? What do you want of me?"

Now had to be the time. She couldn't put it off any longer.

"There *is* something I want," Annie confessed.

She shifted legs, folded them under her, then turned to face Emma Rose. Clasping palms together above her thighs, she looked as if in prayer. Her gaze became acute, her tone intense. "I came here today," Annie said, "because I have something to ask of you."

Her voice carried no apology, sounding almost rehearsed. "But first, I want to tell you how I came to this. When I first took a look at the suit you filed, I was angry, Emma Rose. Most people would be, I guess. But then I became ... well, scared. I didn't have the means to fight a suit. Or pay if I were found guilty in a court of law. Or even to pay a settlement. I didn't even have the money to hire an attorney. But I *wanted* to fight you. Everything depended on it. I didn't know how ..." She looked helplessly at her hands. "Then it came to me I'd be my own lawyer."

"Why are you telling me this?"

"Yes, it came to me," Annie said, ignoring her question, "I'd be my own attorney. I'd do my own ... investigation." And then her full attention focused on Emma Rose. "I went around asking people about you. What kind of person you were. What kind of reputation you had. Were you a drunk? I imagined I'd find something I could use. Maybe you tripped over the wine bottles because you were sloshed before you even entered my shop. Maybe you were ... how to say? ... incompetent, careless, so it wouldn't be too farfetched to believe you weren't watching where you were going. Anything — instability could explain it — your flying in a rage like that ... over absolutely nothing ... attacking Leo ... storming out. Maybe you were crazy. I was desperate. I had a lot at stake. If I lost the suit, I'd be in debt for the rest of my life, and I had other obligations, not only to myself. I had to win. I wasn't going to run from anything anymore. I was sick and tired of that. Crazy fed up with that. And if I were to win, I had to show reasonable doubt as to my own negligence and evidence of your ... blame."

Annie sounded as if she were pleading, begging her to understand. And then she saw the words she spoke so fervently had come to no good end. Emma Rose struggled to get up. She maneuvered her thick thighs off the sheet, clumsily, hastily pressing the palms of her hands against the sheet to support her rise. And when she finally got to her knees — her round belly on full display, the fat forming ripples down the silhouette of her torso, so that Annie became fascinated, taking in the fullness of her buttocks, the blue veins in her plump legs, the flabbiness of her inner arm — she lifted one foot triumphantly and then the other and stared defiantly at Annie: "I don't have to listen to this."

"Please ..."

"No! Who do you think you are? You're an *idiot*," Emma Rose scolded, cheeks turning florid. She yanked up the sheet, shaking it hard so that cracker crumbs and apple cores scattered to the grass. She pressed the bundle to her chest and reached to pick up a knapsack then the book. It was the complete works of Shakespeare.

"No, wait! *I won't bother you again!*"

Emma Rose's lips parted, her eyes betraying myriad emotions, not so much anger this time, for that had been replaced by repugnance and something peculiarly resembling shame. Chin in, lips pressed, Emma Rose turned and fled toward the mansions bordering the park. Annie called after her, "Russell ... he has a message for you ..."

Emma Rose halted, stood with her back to her, before turning in Annie's direction, astonishment in her eyes. The show of disbelief never wavered as the old woman stared at Annie, and then Emma Rose turned again and proceeded toward the stately homes on Exposition Boulevard, walking stiffly, heavily, still with a slight limp. She made her way along the sidewalk in the direction of the river, destined, Annie knew from past observation, for the river side of Magazine Street, where she'd likely turn left on Laurel Street and trudge toward a small cottage that was her home behind a terra cotta mansion.

The cottage was blue. It resembled an Acadian except that Annie believed it wasn't one. It contained a spacious porch with rectangular columns extending all the way around the right side. The doors and shutters were of unvarnished oak; two ceiling fans whirred on the porch. The front steps were brick, the yard a jungle of tropical plants and shrubbery. Annie had seen Emma Rose once, sitting in her spot in the park. Not intentionally, but by chance. She'd followed her from a distance, to this very same cottage. She'd wanted to know more about the woman who was suing her and, later, much later, when her entire world collapsed, when all the misfortune and devastation conspired to overwhelm her, she began thinking about Nehemiah and Leo and where they might live and who might take care of them and she began thinking about this cottage and how they could be happy here. And a crazy desire was born — an insane, bizarre compulsion.

Now, Annie couldn't let her go, couldn't let this chance be lost.

She ran. "*Please … Emma Rose!*"

Amazingly, when she caught up, Emma Rose made no effort to get away. Neither did she turn to face her. Instead, she stood with head bowed in a posture of defeat, shoulders hunched, a paragon of world-angst, looking for the first time, Annie thought, more afraid than anything. Before Annie could speak, Emma Rose got in the first word.

"You tell Russell I have no interest in him."

An iron bench faced the park. Annie walked over, hoping Emma Rose would follow, and wasn't disappointed. She and Emma Rose sat facing the ancient oaks under the shadow of the high branches reaching out like giant arms. Farther off, geese huddled in groups along the banks of the lagoon, white, yellow-white and brown, their coats clean, bellies swollen. A squirrel sat on his hind legs, nibbling on an acorn, white belly and feather-like projections sticking up above a winding tail. He scurried off.

"I found out things I didn't expect," Annie said matter-of-factly. "You won a prize in '73, top prize in a short story contest in McCall's magazine. Way to go, Emma Rose. You're a writer, I always knew that. You love books too much not to be one."

"Not necessarily," Emma Rose snapped.

"How's that?"

"People who love literature aren't necessarily writers."

"Well …" Annie hurried on, "and I found out something else. You were a foster mom to a bunch of kids. Now that was kind of surprising."

Emma Rose scowled.

Annie hastened to go on. "I spoke to one of your neighbors. Miss Josephine Parker. She goes to Our Lady of Guadalupe Church, just like you. She said she'd see you at Mass with those orphaned boys — teens, most of them born in the projects. The ones with the worse histories.

Incorrigible, unadoptable, that's how she described them. Anyway, you took them in. Never boasted about it or tried to impress anyone. Josephine — she'd sit behind you at Mass. They'd sit next to you, those boys, fairly obedient in the beginning, and then they'd start acting up. It amused the hell out of her; you were like a drill sergeant at boot camp. One of them, Russell, he once got up to leave when folks were getting up to go to Holy Communion and she heard you say: 'You know better than that!' The whole church heard: '*You know better than that!* You don't *leave* before Communion.'

"Russell, he was stubborn. He started walking out, like any hard-headed sixteen-year-old. And then you stampeded down that aisle after him, and he got nearly to the door, when you grabbed his arm and forced him back. Made him sit with the others till Mass was over. Miss Josephine said that made her day. She was quite impressed with you. You made a fan, Emma Rose. She said, 'Emma Rose never took no shit.'"

"Woman has a potty mouth."

"Well, Russell didn't like it."

"A collision of two planets." Emma Rose brought the sheet to her face, dabbed at the sweat beading her brow. It was the first day of July. She shielded her eyes from the sun's rays then looked forlornly into the distance. "Good riddance." She lay the sheet on her lap, took a thermos from out of the knapsack, raised the cup to her lips and drank. She didn't offer it to Annie.

"Where did you say he was?"

"I didn't."

"Well then, where is he?"

"Baltimore."

"I see." Emma Rose sat back, staring miserably into the park. And then, as if succumbing to the heat, her words spewed out in a massive tumble of lament: "I always wondered about that."

141

"He was easy to find." Annie said pointedly. "You could have found him."

"Why would I want to do that?"

"To check on him."

"He can go to hell for all I care."

"Emma Rose, you don't mean that."

Emma Rose got up, held the crumpled sheet to her breasts. With brisk determination, she stepped to the back of the bench and waved the sheet vigorously, letting the farthest edges fall to the ground. She began folding it, pairing off corners, till it became a small, neat, rectangular bundle, accomplished in swift, efficient motions. She moved slightly.

"He turned out badly." Emma Rose's voice was strong, but the hurt in it still lingered. "Now, excuse me. I have made plans." She dabbed at her lips, glancing in the direction of the park. It was the loneliness in her eyes that got to Annie.

"Wait," Annie hurried on. "Don't you want to hear the message?"

"Don't care, my dear."

"He's a hot shot lawyer." Annie spoke quickly. "A legislator. What do you think of that?"

"What nerve you have intruding on my life."

"You sued me, Emma Rose."

"I dropped it."

"You did what?"

"You heard me."

Annie got up, searching for the right words and finding none, stammered, "Why?"

"Why what?"

"Did you drop the suit?"

The only other time Annie had been with Emma Rose, the old woman carried herself with pride. To Annie, pure arrogance bounced off her, while others might call it belligerence. Now, before her, none of that was evident: the disdain, resentment, haughtiness. Instead, radiating from her was a troubled single-mindedness, a no-nonsense desire to take care of unfinished business. Emma Rose stepped grimly to the front of the bench, put down the knapsack, and dropped the book on the seat. She took her time sitting down, wearily but with purpose. Annie noticed the wrinkles for the first time, the cat's-claws shooting out in deep trenches around the eyes, the stooped posture, rounded shoulders: a defeated old woman with loose skin hanging from the neck.

"I started thinking about it. I caused it," Emma Rose said softly. She seemed to have forgotten her distaste and bitterness and the words came spilling out. "I may be a lot of things, but dishonest with myself I'm not. I caused it. It came to me in the middle of the night. My leg was itching under the cast and my arm was aching and I was furious over what happened, filled with hatred for the whole lot of you. Do you have any idea how helpless a woman feels with a broken leg and arm? It was past three in the morning. I couldn't sleep, my leg itched; I couldn't scratch it. And do you know what? Some quiet voice announced itself above my aggravation and descended upon me. And then I realized the voice wasn't descending but coming from inside of me. And I thought about it, really thought about it.

"It had been storming that night then all was calm," she went on. "I could hear rain sporadically dropping from the redbud tree outside my bedroom window and hit the grass as if everything was almost over. It was cool, everything quiet, I realized it was my fault. I provoked the man. He did the only thing he could to get rid of me. Take flight toward the bottles. Ease his pain, I suppose, with … what was it you served? … La Vieille Ferme and Oak Grove Pinot Noir? You see, I'm not such a forgetful old turkey as they make me out to be. Those … detestable farts at the library. Over forty years I worked there …"

Annie did not interrupt.

Emma Rose stared at a yellow lab chasing a squirrel up a tree. The dog trotted back to its master, one of four middle-aged women chatting happily on the sidewalk to the far right of Emma Rose. He joined two others on leashes poking their heads in the grass.

Beyond the women, a dazzling sight: a tree. A purple tree. As tall as a house with tiny violet leaves, like a million dots upon the landscape. Annie watched as Emma Rose stared, mesmerized, and imagined she might be thinking how radiant was its color blended with the surrounding foliage, blossomy magnolias and angel's trumpets and birds-of-paradise, and how startling, in the midst of all, a hundred feet from the mansions, this graceful tree with its million buds of violet.

Emma Rose turned back to Annie.

"I can't take too much provocation. People provoke me and I fight back. They kicked me out of the only job I ever had. Forty years I worked there. Faithful and loyal. Nobody could be more loyal. And conscientious ... I kept it all inside and, finally, exploded — at him." She paused. "What did you say his name was?"

"Leo."

"Leo — that's right. Oh, yes. Leo Tolstoy, he called himself. That's what he said his name was." Her tone grew earnest. "I caused it. And the voice told me."

"What did it say?"

"'Drop the suit, Emma Rose.'"

"The voice said that?"

"'Those people did nothing to you'. As clear as I'm talking now. The voice telling me the truth. And I realized it was coming from within. I took a few days to mull it over. And then I realized it was right. And I wanted to tell you in person — tell you I was going to drop the suit. I even came to your shop one night, the night of the prisoners' readings. I took a cab and went to that expense because I wanted to sit face to face with you and apologize. You cannot imagine how awful it was with a broken leg and arm hobbling on my crutch to deliver the message to you in person. Or the nightmare of that barbarian attacking me at the door. But I'm not going to stoop to name calling. She threw me out like I was trash. Then I read in the paper what happened to you, the shooting in your shop. And then the shop closed and I asked my attorney not to pursue it and forgot about it after that."

"There's no suit?"

"None."

"*Oh my God* ..." Annie's voice lifted as she contemplated this unexpected turn of events. She waited for relief, some rare rush of happiness, and it came and it went, and there was emptiness after that. "I'm glad," Annie said gratefully. "I couldn't have paid it if you'd won." She crossed her legs, staring into the distance. She turned back to Emma Rose. "But that's not why I came, to tell you to drop the suit. I came for another reason. Do you want to hear what he said?"

"Who?"

"Russell. He told me you saved his life." She let that sink in. "He didn't think much of you when he left. You two argued all the time. But he said that things you'd say would come back to haunt him at different stages of his life. Like 'Think twice before accusing anyone.' Or 'Never assume anything — always ask.' And how you never gave up finding answers to his homework problems — little things. He said you once stayed up all night trying to solve a bonus question in one of his classes. That blew his mind, Emma Rose. He never forgot about it. And as much as he thought he hated you, you instilled that in him."

"What?"

"Never give up."

"I thought he might have died from a botched crack deal."

"Emma Rose, that's enough."

145

*

Emma Rose stared angrily. And then her mind wandered back to the last time she'd awakened Russell. Russell Walker was his name. She couldn't believe how long ago it had been; almost twenty years had passed. Emma Rose tucked in her chin. She'd been good to that bratty boy. She'd fight anybody who dared say otherwise. Why, she remembered something that happened, a shared moment with her boys.

She'd taken them to a St. Patrick's Day parade to celebrate Russell's sixteenth birthday. They'd wandered down Magazine Street in the Irish Channel and the street was splashed in green paint. A costumed band of marchers lined up in front of St. Andrew's Babies Asylum, a four-story brick structure enclosed by an iron fence and, stretching across the fence, the marchers draped a yellow banner, "Sultans of Music Marching Band." The sultans' musicians were warming up, playing a get-down strutting-funky beat, and the sultans were swinging their hips while swilling green beer in paper cups. Her boys — Clay, Reginald, Russell, and Dujon — were having the time of their young lives, watching a lone dancer, a black man in the street. Hips swaying, arm raised, the dancer jabbed his finger toward the sky, the other arm down, finger pointed to the street, one foot forward then back, other forward then back, shoulders shimmying, head moving; he held it together with dexterity and magnificent skill, supremely confident, grooving, moving smoothly, yet jerkily to accentuate the rhythm, cool as a cucumber, having fun with a controlled ease.

Russell and her other boys found him infectious. Russell strutted over to within a few feet of the man and swayed his hips in time with his, his expression dead pan, ironic, eyes brimming with good time. He was a born dancer. And confident, that Russell. Could do anything, go anywhere, his future dazzling, Emma Rose recalled. Her other boys followed him into the street.

Then the floats began to move. They were large, covered on all sides with a green grassy material. The floats rolled between marchers in black tuxedos, politicos atop convertibles tossing beads and doubloons, trucks loaded with musicians playing *Won't You Come Home, Bill Bailey?*, the crowd starting to go wild, rushing to within inches of the floats to catch what was being offered by ladies with bleached hair and middle-aged, balding fellows. Her boys were running too, throwing up their hands to collect cabbages and carrots, onions and cucumbers. Some of the male marchers, spotting a pretty girl, would dance up to her in the street, pick out a green paper flower from a Styrofoam box of flowers, and hand one to the girl and kiss her on the lips before dancing back into the parade.

Emma Rose recalled when she had been young and pretty and a marcher picking her out of a crowd and giving her a flower and kissing her on the lips before heading back to his group and others coming up afterwards, till she'd been loaded down with flowers. That had been years ago, before she'd taken on her boys. Back then, a young man had appeared, a stranger but very handsome, to invite her to his party and kiss her on the lips then disappear into the crowd but not before giving her his name and address and how loved she'd felt back then in her wild and promising youth.

There were many men back then. But as the years drifted on, they suddenly stopped calling. It's strange how age crept up and how the body fell apart and all the men mysteriously vanished. No dates. No romance. No men. There were no longer even parade marchers to dance up to her in the street to kiss her on the lips and give her paper flowers.

But these boys of hers were running to give her all their loot. And she would take them home to make beef stew and bake a carrot cake and have a party in celebration of Russell's sixteenth birthday. She would never again be beautiful and her youth was long gone and the romances of the past over. But she had her boys — her rambunctious boys. And there was much to do for them and she could be happy with that. Emma Rose looked up to find herself back in Audubon Park. "I did the best I could ...," she groaned.

*

Emma Rose looked vaguely disoriented, or so it appeared to Annie. The old woman stared into the park before turning her attention to Annie. Emma Rose's eyes lingered on her an inordinate amount of time, but not seeing her, Annie realized. Still, Annie could feel the longing in them, the helplessness and uncontrollable anger, as if she were frantic to defend herself, defend the image of the person she thought she was, that flash of defiance and unbearable sadness and longing making it difficult for Annie to bring up the question she had come here to ask. Emma Rose looked defeated.

"The last morning I went into Russell's room," Emma Rose declared, settling back and sighing, "it was surreally quiet. I wasn't used to that with my boys. There was always ... action ... in my house, even when they were supposed to be asleep. You never knew what trouble they were getting into, taking a match to the curtains, a switchblade to each other. And then there was ..." She stopped and, to Annie's dismay, tears appeared in her eyes, "... no child in bed. I never saw him after that."

"You missed him?" Annie asked.

"Missed *things*. Cranberry muffins baking in the oven with him sitting at the kitchen table, then watching him gobble it down. That's when we had our best talks. It wasn't all fights, you know. Missed struggling with his homework and having that pay ... dividends. You know, Russell was bright. Too bright to be ruined by that hellhole school system. I worked with all my children equally. But Russell was ... exceptional. I wanted all of them to raise their heads above the mud. To live good lives. But I thought if anyone could ... truly triumph ... surely it would be him."

Emma Rose pressed the sheet to her chest. Her head tilted to one side as she closed her eyes. She sat in silence, sheet tight against her. And then she let go. She looked out into the park and Annie looked where she looked, at the jogging path straight ahead, as a black woman belted out at the top of her lungs, "... I am not afraid ... after all that I've been through ..." moving shoulders and arms for emphasis, forging speedily ahead. Emma Rose's tone was bitter. "That was a long time ago."

"And you changed."

"Says who?"

"Miss Josephine."

"Oh, of course."

"She said you took in no kids after that. That you lost your patience and ... your humanity."

"Obnoxious frog."

Emma Rose sat up, chin jutting out, nails digging into the soft flesh of her arm.

"Where did you say he was?" Emma Rose murmured.

"Baltimore."

"And what's he doing?"

"After he ran away," Annie answered, "he thought of you, he said. But in a bad way — all the times you forced him to go to Mass and wouldn't let him hang with his drug buddies. Or the time you caught him and his pals smoking weed behind the parking lot when you came to sit in on one of his classes, and how you told the principal, and they suspended him. You taught him at home after that, till he got back in school — and he hated you. Absolutely hated you. But after a time, he began to remember good things.

149

He said everything you taught him played in his favor. You were in his head, Emma Rose. He couldn't get you out. There'd be Emma Rose telling him not to fraternize with the thugs, Emma Rose telling him to get off his butt and work. Despite himself, he became what you wanted. And you know what? This is what he became: a politician. A state legislator. You probably think that's funny. He has a private law practice as well. He said to tell you he's honest. And though he didn't know it at the time he left, he loved you, Emma Rose. And he told me to thank you."

Tears streamed down Emma Rose's face and her cheeks were bright red. Haltingly, she placed a hand over the book. Her voice broke. Her hand trembled. "Why didn't *he* tell me?"

"He was ashamed. A lot of time passed. He got busy. You know how things go. He said he thought of contacting you over the years, but the more he thought about how he treated you the more ashamed he became. It got harder over time. He told me to tell you this: everything good he did in his life, it was because of you. And it would be an honor and a privilege if you would let him take you out some day. He said he'd fly down and see you. Would that be something you might like, Emma Rose?"

Emma Rose turned completely away, looking fiercely at the sidewalk. She wiped her eyes, focusing her attention on an ant zigzagging toward her foot. Annie cleared her throat. "You think about it. And let me know. And now I'd like to tell you why I came. I have something to ask of you: Will you take Nehemiah?"

Emma Rose looked at her.

"He doesn't need much," Annie hurried on. "He's the kind of child who could take care of himself. He's so good, Emma Rose. But he's only ten and he needs food and a clean bed to sleep in. And someone who might love him, of course. And, you know ..." she continued eagerly, "you two have a lot in common. He's interested in writing. He has a literary talent but the schools in this city won't do him any good, so you could teach him grammar and punctuation ... and ... you'd be wonderful at that ..."

Annie fidgeted, her voice fading. "I thought of a lot of folks who might be suitable. Father Rigoli might know parishioners who could give him a good home. There are people with means who might take on that responsibility. But I couldn't get you out of my mind after talking with Russell. I needed someone who cared. That's the least I can do for him. He's the most beautiful —"

"I'm afraid I don't understand."

"I don't have much time."

Emma Rose sat up and moved a little away. It was a reflexive move, Annie thought, not intended to be unkind. After awhile, Emma Rose said carefully: "I don't think I understand. You want me to take a child? What child are you thinking of? I saw one the day of the discussion group — the boy who ran to Leo. Is that who you're referring to?"

"Yes. His name is Casimier. Nehemiah Casimier. His mom's dead and his dad ..." Annie shrugged. "The grandma was taking care of him and, after she passed, I took over. But I will be leaving soon. It could be any time."

"Why ..." Emma Rose's eyes widened, "... this is most unusual. Am I to assume you're going away somewhere?"

"I'm dying, Emma Rose."

Emma Rose placed the palm of her hand against her wet cheek before dropping it in her lap. "Excuse me," she said formally, "my memory isn't good. Did you say you were sick when you first approached?"

"A repetition disorder."

"I see." Emma Rose paused. "No, I don't see ..."

"It doesn't matter."

"I want to know."

"I have a form of dementia."

"Alzheimer's?" she stammered. "You're young. People my age ... I'm much more —"

"It's not that," Annie interrupted. "What I have you can get at 40. It happens to people between 40 and 64. I'm 51. I fit right in."

"Does it have a name?"

"It does."

"What is it?"

"It doesn't matter."

"I insist ..."

"Emma Rose ..." Annie took a deep breath and pondered how to proceed. She hadn't wanted to get into this, though she knew dodging it would be impossible. She took another deep breath, placed her hand over her forehead, then plunged right in, her tone deliberately matter-of-fact. "Frontotemporal dementia. Some people call it Pick's Disease. There isn't much time. My doctor," she said, swallowing, "he says I have less than a week — more likely a few days — before I reach the late stage."

"How does he know?"

"He took a brain scan."

"And then?"

"A loss of speech. Then I'll become mute. A loss of muscle movement. Then I'll be unable to move. Death will come from the complications of that."

Annie crossed her legs, letting her foot dangle. Her voice was nearly cheerful. "I was told to get my things in order. But that hasn't been easy since most days I don't know what's going on." She smiled. "That's a hell of a position to be in, don't you think? Today, I woke up feeling good. I could think. I could recognize objects. I knew today was the day I had to talk to you."

Annie folded her arms and squinted into the sun. "I have to make plans. I can't put it off. I could wake up tomorrow and all the symptoms would be back: the crazy behavior, taking off my clothes. Honestly, I did that — right in the Winn Dixie. The doing obsessive things, like collecting food and dumping them in a cart … Today was good. I knew when I woke up, you and I would have this talk. Tomorrow …" her voice trailed off.

"When did this … happen?" Emma Rose looked frightened.

There was a stump of a tree, with a jagged edge, near a clump of tall weeds, and Annie focused on that. It was a little before the jogging path where a couple roller skated. She heard the jabber of far off children, a bird squawking and flying off. She felt a breeze, mild, not hot. "I guess … let's see … I began noticing things after Zella died. I'd sit with Leo trying to make sense of things and couldn't … I couldn't focus. I thought I was going nuts trying to put the sequence of events in order. I thought I'd lost my mind. I dismissed it as the natural consequence of all I'd been through. Shock, grief. After all, I'd lost my business and then my best friend. Zella — she was the boy's grandma … And then there was Leo. And the boy, Feayo." She glanced wistfully at her companion. She stopped and leaned back. "Leo, I wish you could have known him, Emma Rose. You didn't really know him. It was a lot to take in. In time I thought I'd be my old self …"

"And that didn't happen?"

Annie looked abstractedly into the park then up at the vibrant sky. She stood up, wiped off the back of her skirt, then carefully sat down again. "I developed this … yen for food," she said. "I'd eat anything I could get my hands on. And that's probably why I piled all that food into the cart. I was going to take it home and eat it — all by myself. You see, Nehemiah … he explained to me … told me what I'd been doing. He was most concerned and worried … he wanted to know why …

"But that wasn't the worst of it," she went on. "I've been so cruel to Leo. You see, his brain is damaged, his visual span so limited he can't see an entire word. He has to learn to read letter by letter. Then he has to remember what the letter means and then the word and sometimes he forgets before he goes on to the next word. This is ... an impossible task. But he doesn't give up. He gives it everything he's got. Someone like that needs a lot of *support*. A lot of attention. I couldn't give it to him, Emma Rose. I've been so indifferent."

"Why?"

"It has to do with what I've got. The doctor said near the final stage I'll become indifferent. Apathetic. Then limited in my speech. And then I'll become mute."

"You seem all right. There doesn't seem to be anything —"

"I woke up and my head was clear. I was lucid. He said this is to be expected. It won't last. Dr. Shea, my doctor, says there'll be problems in swallowing, in breathing —"

"Get another doctor, for Christ's sake! *Get another opinion.* What's he trying to do?"

"Prepare me, Emma Rose. There's no treatment —"

"You don't know —"

"I do."

"Prepare you for what?"

"Death. The disease progresses quickly. There'll be clear days then everything will go down fast. I'll lose the control of my motor functions. That's why I knew I couldn't put it off. That's why I'm here ... *will you take him, Emma Rose?*"

"You can't just give away a boy," Emma Rose stammered. "Why, dear Lord, there are procedures and courts and social-service agencies involved. You can't just give away a *child* like you'd dish out a bowl of gumbo —"

"*What am I supposed to do?*" Annie shot back. "Give him to Community Services, who'll give him to his *father?* He just got out of jail on drug charges. I investigated that. I'd rather send him to Siberia than give him to his father.

Throw away his life like that. *Please,* Emma Rose, his dad doesn't give a damn. Never tried to visit. Please ... consider ... I'm begging you to *consider!*"

Emma Rose didn't answer. Annie felt ashamed; she didn't mean to go on and on. She composed herself, stood up, searching for whatever would be her last words. "I know it's a surprise. Things don't happen the way we expect. And none of us is prepared to deal with it. For a long time you wish it'd be a nightmare and you'd wake up. But you don't. Maybe I've grown up. A year ago, I'd probably have killed myself. At the very least, run away. I'm very good at that. But today ..." Annie shrugged, "I knew I had to come to you. I wouldn't bother you if it wasn't important. I know you'll need time. You don't have to tell me right this minute ..." She tried smiling but her expression turned oddly grotesque, her mouth strangely foolish. She continued in a shaky voice: "Tomorrow, if everything's right, I'll meet you here at the same time. *The very same time, Emma Rose?*"

Emma Rose didn't look up. Annie thought she saw her nod or maybe it was her imagination. Annie turned and headed toward St. Charles Avenue, trying to be hopeful. Emma Rose might say yes. It might take a few days, there might be a chance. This is, after all, a woman bent on control, who thrives on complications, is addicted to process, any process, Annie knew, but especially one that's right. And what could be more right than taking Nehemiah? And she is an energetic woman with time on her hands. If Annie could think of another person willing to take on such a task, but she was sorry to admit she was coming up short, and there wasn't enough time, and Emma Rose topped the list. Pitiful, you might say. *But there is more to Emma Rose than anybody knows.* And besides, Nehemiah will keep her straight. He was one full grown human being masquerading as a child. All he needed was a place to grow, a clean and tidy room and food that will nourish him. Emma Rose could give him that. She could read to him the good stories, share her love of books …

And Annie couldn't let herself get too frantic over Leo. She needed to ask Emma Rose if she might take Leo too. But she would broach that subject at a more opportune time — tomorrow, it would have to be. Now would be disastrous. And Emma Rose would either take him or she wouldn't. There was nothing more she could do. Besides, Nehemiah wouldn't desert Leo. And if worse came to worse and Annie ran out of time before anything could be resolved, Father Rigoli would take over.

And she must remember tomorrow to tell her what Nehemiah's teacher said, how gifted Nehemiah was, with a vivid imagination and extraordinary memory and that he showed an unusual interest in words. And how she'd raved about how quickly he learned and what a whiz he was at math and how independent and resilient; she must remember to tell her that, and then Emma Rose would be hooked on the similarities between him and the young Russell, the connection ripe with possibilities — possibilities for a second chance. Surely she'd want a second chance.

And maybe his grammar wasn't perfect — not surprising, considering the way he was brought up (taken out of school, imprisoned at his mama's place). And it was a miracle he didn't suffer brain damage from his lack of stimuli. And it was a testament to his great tenacity to live through all of that and still be as smart as he was; she must remember to tell her that.

Something else she must tell her once she'd agreed to take Leo, a secret she has carried and must now give up. "He's not what you think," she'd say, "but a man of great talent and you must protect it and cherish it." Then she'd tell her his real name was Marvin Everillo and of the masterpiece he created and she would bestow upon her the great honor to get *Faulkner & Friends* published. Emma Rose, a former librarian, would know what to do, Annie didn't have the slightest doubt. She'd bulldoze it through to press, not that she would ever need to. The greatest forces in Leo's life, this woman's stubbornness and his talent, would combine to set the world on fire, but Annie wouldn't be around to see it.

XIV. copiosa apud eum redemptio

Annie hustled to meet the streetcar. She climbed on board, took a seat on the side nearest to the park, watched Emma Rose in the far distance still sitting in the same spot, face rigid, eyes downcast, as if hypnotized by the moving ant. Annie turned to look across the aisle at the sprawling campuses of the universities. The streetcar began to roll, taking her past Napoleon and Louisiana and Josephine, where she'd intended to get off. Instead, she sat passively taking in the sights till she reached the foot of Canal.

She got off at Canal and took a bus to Esplanade.

And when the bus was nearest the gates of the cemetery, that's when she got off. She made her way to the statue, stood in front of Padre Pio's outstretched arms, and there he was staring back. He was not like Francis Seelos. There was more authority in his expression. He wore a beard, a mustache, and, if he could speak, his voice would be powerful, guiding her through this with utmost confidence. *What is it, Padre Pio? Tell me what you're telling me.* But the only sounds came from the street, and from the birds in the playground beyond. She looked at the plaque beneath Padre Pio's feet and even this did not speak to her. And because it was noisy in the cemetery — a line of cars moving on the black pavement to get to the entrance then out to the Boulevard, and because she felt watched and humiliated by being watched as she stood before the Friar — she quickly departed, making her way to another destination.

Mother Teresa was a football's throw away from where Padre Pio stood. But where there'd once been tall grass obscuring the epigraph beneath her feet, there now was a patch of daisies. Teresa's eyes did not meet Annie's. They seemed to be glancing to the right of her. But they weren't looking at anything at all, really. Teresa's thoughts were somewhere else. She was smiling, totally caught up in the rhapsody of her own joy. Mother, speak to me. But she was wholly engrossed, absorbed in some sweet pleasure, the rosary in her hand. So Annie looked down at the words: "If you pray, you will have faith. And if you have faith, you will love. If you love, you will serve. And if you serve, you will find peace." Annie considered how the nun once served, the deaths and stench and misery all around her. And yet, she'd seen Mother Teresa once on TV. How humble she looked. Humble and satisfied. Glad and content, tolerating the archbishop who fell all over himself asking dumb questions. Tolerating him in the most joyous, humble way.

Peace somehow eluded Annie, lost somewhere in the process. And faith, what was that? Zella had faith. Totally convinced that somehow Father Seelos would right every wrong and become a saint with one more miracle and somehow save the world — save her and Zella and Leo and Nehemiah and Feayo. And here she was, about to die in some disgusting, hideous manner and Zella dead after her grandson shot himself after setting fire to a building and killing a man, and how terrible was their fate, none of them could ever imagine in the bleakest moment of their lives, and poor Seelos in his grave after succumbing to yellow fever, expected to rise up and right every wrong in a pyrotechnic display of almighty power and righteousness.

Hallelujah ... praise be .... How pathetic was hope. Father Rigoli told a story once, at the Sunday Mass of Epiphany. He told the story of the star that the three Wisemen followed to lead them to the Christ child. He said a little boy once suggested that the star be broken up into tiny pieces that would become a million silver twinklers. The child said a twinkler should be placed in the eye of every newborn so that when people looked into their eyes they could see Jesus shining there, a light to give them hope.

Once, she'd had hope. She'd written in her diary when she was a little girl, "Everything that is beautiful is based on hope. And whatever it is I believe in, it has not let me down." That diary meant so much to her she'd wanted to keep it in a safe place, away from prying eyes, so she buried it in the back yard and never found it after that. So much for childhood, everything in black and white.

She knew she wasn't ready to leave this world. After all, she'd made so many plans. All the people she'd help, make a difference on this earth. Here in this city, it was a peculiar thing, really, how long-time businesses were cherished as families. Loved, when it was time to go. She remembered the messages taped to the door of a popular grill close to the universities that had closed after its owner absconded and never came back. *Open up ... I'm begging you ... I'm crazy for your cherry pie!*

She'd thought maybe she'd get through the rough times in the first year of operation then go about the task of achieving her high goals: the poetry readings and book discussions and writing contests and signings, maybe sit with a child awhile and tutor him in private, mentor him till the whole world discovered his shining talent, was that too much to ask? Was it too much to ask to take pride in one's work? She'd thought her store would be a sacred ground for the city's undiscovered talent, a place for the lost to find their reason to live, a masterpiece rising out of the ashes of their flaming lives, all because of *Faulkner & Friends* and the magic she'd created out of faith and hope. What in the world happened? Why did it end so badly?

Was it because there was nothing to believe in and dreams are never realized? Or because she hadn't used good sense, at the least raised enough capital to stay in business awhile? Or maybe work in a bookshop, get the experience before starting out. Little things. She remembered when the dream had come. She'd been 18, a college kid fresh from her parents' home, come to live in a dorm, in a small school run by the nuns.

She was a freshman and one day she took a streetcar to Royal Street to mess around in the Quarter, all excited to be free and wild in the big city. And she happened to walk into a used bookstore. It was tiny, long, and narrow. The proprietor, his name was Al, stood behind a counter, smiling. He offered her a drink of vodka. And they became trusted and loyal friends. Faithfully, every Saturday morning, she'd hop over to Al's bookshop and he'd offer her a Screwdriver and there'd be a dozen other's hanging out: Babe Stoval, the blues guitarist, he always wandered in, and professors from Tulane and Loyola, they'd stop in and chat, and strangers from out of town, tourists; it was the most exciting, intoxicating, beautiful, and wonderful place. Al's bookshop. But, come to think of it, she couldn't remember seeing anybody buy a book. How did he manage to make a living? He had two kids. He'd once been a lawyer in a small Alabama town. How did he survive?

Young and dreamy, she never thought about those things then. It was just that, as time passed, she'd always wanted what he had: the freedom and companionship and discussions about world affairs. Simple as that. A salon, where she would be the beloved hostess, a community where she belonged, like Gertrude Stein's in the rue de Fleurus, a compulsion — addiction — born in that great shop, a dream, with no concern for the nitty-gritty details of making money.

Stop it right now, feeling sorry for yourself.

She didn't have time to dwell on sad memories. Nehemiah and Leo, she had to think of them. What a lucky woman she'd become for having them in her life. To be given a second chance. And ever since their arrival, her world had completely changed.

They needed her, confided. Take Leo, for instance. Surely, he was private, but he told her things he never told anyone. He said someone asked him once at the signing for *Second-Story Window* why he writes about the things he writes about. He said he doesn't write about it, something leads him and he follows. Sometimes he'll read what he wrote and

161

ask himself why he couldn't write something funny. Or why did he have to go into that maudlin subject? And he often thought if he'd written what he wanted to write, it would be a completely different novel than what was written by the thing he followed. Was that thing the Muse? Was it the Holy Ghost, the Blessed Trinity, Higher Power? Was it God — all those things God? If so, what was God?

One day he'd find out, find the answer to who was leading him when he wrote the best he could (when he went on his own determined path the work turned out a mess), and one day he'd know who led him up the stairs to the attic where all the treasures were, one day he'd find out. One day. Now that was in Annie's hands. Someone to take care of him.

Nehemiah had his own ghosts. He blamed himself for Feayo's death. She asked him once what had happened when he was with his cousin moments before he died and he never really answered, and she could understand why. Then one day he confided. It came out of nowhere. They were packing in the front room. She was sitting down, dazed, gazing into space as she often did. Sometimes she felt so shocked over everything that happened she could only sit and stare, just stay that way till the mood reversed itself. And she felt someone's hand on her. She looked over; it was Nehemiah. He was crying, sitting on the floor beside her. She reached out, drew him near. It was shortly after all the deaths. And they stayed that way, holding on, and then he told her about the moment before Feayo shot himself.

This is what Feayo told him: he didn't just happen to go over with a box of matches in his hand. No, when he saw the door open, he tiptoed back to where they'd been sleeping and took a can of lighter fluid and a roll of paper towels. He entered the door across the street, advanced up the stairs and slipped strips of paper part way under the doors, then took a match to the soaked paper and stood there, waiting. He wanted to be sure. And when things went the way he wanted, he fled down the stairs. He heard human screams from the upper level. He turned, a pit bull following him. And that was all. It was easy. But not so easy afterward.

At first, he tried convincing himself that what he did was good. That he'd killed the man who killed his dad, that what he did was justified. But the mind has a way of cutting through all the crap and it didn't take long before the truth revealed itself, shocking him with its intensity, hounding him without mercy till he could not deny it or run away: that despite what that man did he had a right to be alive. That not only did he kill a man he hated, he turned the gun on a man he loved, even love couldn't stop him, and this was the thing that turned his stomach, would do it over and over and over again. He was nothing but a rabid dog. There was nothing else to say. And only one thing to do about it.

There was silence after that. They got up and packed. What else was there to do if not the next thing ahead of them? Leo taught her that. Leo and Nehemiah, they were counting on her. What she must do in the time remaining was find them a home, someone Nehemiah could talk to, someone to guide him and love him. Put Leo's mind at ease, help him suffer less. He'd never figure out the difference between the Holy Ghost and Muse, but at least he'd have someone to teach him a word or two.

The thought came to her that if she hadn't taken them in, their lives would have been spared. Zella would be alive. Feayo. That man. Those animals. And Leo, he'd be writing and using that brain of his. He had many years remaining, a future undoubtedly brilliant, if he could only figure out a way to put the cork back in the bottle. And her? What would she be doing if she hadn't taken them in? What would she be doing if she had never opened that failure of a shop? Why, planning one, of course. No one could take that away: a compulsion — obsession — doomed to live in her brain forever.

Another thought: closing the shop was another big mistake. After all, she hadn't been forced to do it. She was only a few weeks late in moving out of the back room. And if she had begged, Mr. Zibilich would have let her stay. They'd already found a place to sleep, which was all he really cared about. No, liquidating had been her idea. She figured she couldn't mind the shop and do what she had to do. Someone had to care for Leo. You couldn't leave a brain-damaged man in the hospital to linger alone. And after he got out, there were a million things he needed. And who else was going to do them? And there were other problems as well.

All her money was gone. Zella died and there had to be a funeral. And Nehemiah didn't want just any funeral, he wanted a jazz funeral for her. And she didn't have it in her heart to tell him she couldn't afford it. So Annie got it together, dressed her in her finest dress, the blue with the yellow flowers, and bought the most beautiful casket, and Father Rigoli got some parishioners to carry her, wearing white gloves and boutonnieres.

And after the funeral, she got a second-line sendoff, with a group of musicians Annie found to play their horns and drums, and the little gathering — the parishioners Zella helped out at the church — danced, white handkerchiefs waving, to the tune *Let Your Mind Be Free* on the way to Zella's old haunts: the bookshop, then her old 'hood, then back to the church again, where Father Rigoli, bless his heart, released a single dove, which flew way up in the sky on its way to its rendezvous with Zella.

And it cost. Every penny. Buried her at Holy Angels, alongside Feayo. Annie even got a horse-drawn hearse to carry her in. And that thrilled Nehemiah. And now she was broke. She could possibly have hung on if not for her stupid spending. She could have found some other way to carry on and not shut down the shop. Then it would have been closed due to illness and not because of failure.

And now, it was gone, but in no way her crazy dream. The great achievement of her life was her longing for a bookshop. And they could laugh and put on her tombstone: *'She kept it open three whole months.'* The tragedy of her life was that she'd dragged them along with her down this dreamy lost path that ended up nowhere. *Stop it! Stop it! Stop tearing yourself apart.* The least she'd wanted was to die looking pretty, not twenty pounds overweight, immobile and helpless and frantic and alone.

But she wouldn't be alone. They would be there. They would stay by her side till death finally came. And so she had to get busy. What she achieved today was for the rest of their lives. *God help me! Get busy ... stay focused ... concentrate ...* But to the right of her, a young man in a bright shirt who looked goofy had turned on a water faucet and was drinking from it and washing his hands. He was taking off his shirt, exposing tattoos all over his back, and giving himself a sponge bath, and the disturbance of the splashing water angered Annie. And when he walked off and left the water pouring onto the blackened pavement, forming a river of wasted water, she could have taken the cane he carried and hit him over the head for wasting the city's water and ruining her concentration. She went over, turned off the spigot, and gave a final glance to the smiling nun and, feeling nothing — absolutely nothing — made her way to Esplanade. She got on a bus for Canal. It no longer was an option to take her own car. God knows where she'd end up. Then she got on a streetcar that took her up St. Charles.

She got off at Josephine.

It was a long walk before reaching the Church. The sky was bathed in lavender. Music from a radio filtered through an open window and she listened to a familiar song, failing to recall the words. And as the final refrain died out, Annie saw her old shop. (Or the window she once loved, that had displayed her favorite books.) But what she saw at that moment were two blue and green T-shirts, one with the legend, "Garden District Babe," the other, "Ninth Ward Hood." The shop next door, once Sophie's Ice Cream, was now a tattoo parlor. A youth, limbs covered in tattoos, stood in front, dragging off a cigarette.

Six o'clock. Mass ended. She entered St. Mary's. Worshippers were streaming out. Annie turned to avoid their faces, settling in a back pew. She was kneeling and her heart was empty. She sat back, looking down. Across her shoes, a rainbow splashed, coming from a stained glass window. She smiled. Zella would have a field day. Annie thought of all the half-crazed notions Zella's deluded heart would dream up. *Father Seelos trying to tell you something, baby.* Annie strained to remember her voice but it never rose above a whisper and quickly died out, so she was aware of the clumsiness of her imagination and longing. What to do? What to do? She kneeled and there was silence and her heart was filled with yearning. *I am fifty-one years old. Is this all I've come to?* Bowed, eyes shut, head bent above her folded hands, she searched for something — anything — to distract her, but all she could think of was Leo and Nehemiah and the unfinished task ahead and the truth she could not escape: too late, too late.

She counted the columns — thirty in all — thick as redwood and rising seven stories tall. *They will get by. It will be done.* She saw the walls, a pale yellow, and the 14-foot tall stained glass and 25 statues of angels surrounding the Blessed Mother in tiers upon the High Altar. What will be done? What did she mean by that? Nehemiah will take care of Leo. Nehemiah will take care of himself. Father will help out, if it comes to that. Stay calm. Think. You don't have much time. She braced herself against the panic. Tonight she will go back and have a talk with Father. He will make some kind of announcement at Mass. There'll be parishioners who'll step forward like angels in the night. Or Catholic Charities will take over. All these doomsday prophesies floating in your head, they are as false and pitiful as your life long ago. Didn't you learn nothing? Zella talking now — clear as the church bells on Sunday morning. You had all these things: You had me and Nehemiah and Leo in your life. And for a precious moment you even had Feayo. And the bookshop, don't forget that. Maybe only for a few months. But there's people in this world who never even had a book — Zella talking again — so don't you go complaining. You did all right, gal. You stop that moaning. And tonight when you go home — Zella again — you make a list of all them things you can do. Get a burger with the boys. Watch a movie on TV. Get yourself some ice cream. Go read a book. Let Nehemiah read to you. And when there's nothing more — you hear me? — let someone else take over. *You done good, gal. Ain't nobody done as good as you. And right now's all you got. It's all anybody ever got.*

The pale rose columns caught her eye and she followed them to the domed ceiling. It was the brightness of her surroundings, the yellow walls, rose columns, the statues of angels — blues and yellows and reds of their robes — and, above them, a round stained-glass in rich greens and reds, and, above that, near the ceiling, a cross surrounded by the words, COPIOSA APUD EUM REDEMPTIO, and it was all of this blended with the golden artwork and pale walls that brought a glorious golden aura, giving the effect of golden otherworldliness and glory and holy splendor. *Blessed Father, intercede for us.*

She stood, made her way down the aisle toward the doors that took her out of the church and past the corner of St. Andrew and Josephine, where men had gathered in the waning light. They were drinking beer and talking as someone rolled a pair of dice on the sidewalk and into the street, and someone's remark brought peals of laughter accompanied by a faint moan, and Annie stopped for a moment, alert to their voices.

SPECIAL THANKS

I wish to thank Lee Meitzen Grue, Julie Kane, James Nolan, and Linda Zoghby Shepler for helping to make my story better. Thanks to Robert Snow for many years of unfailing encouragement. I will forever be grateful to Bill Hoyle whose little bookshop in the French Quarter filled the mind of the college freshman I once was with a love of books and a lifelong devotion to bookstores. Thanks to my wonderful husband, Wayne Holley, for his loving support and advice. And my deepest gratitude goes to Cetywa Powell for believing in my book and giving it the perfect home.

ABOUT VICKI SALLOUM

Born in Gulfport, Mississippi, Vicki Salloum has lived in New Orleans for many years with her husband, Wayne Holley. Her debut novella, *A Prayer to Saint Jude*, was published in 2012 by Main Street Rag Publishing. Her short stories have been included in the anthologies *When I Am An Old Woman I Shall Wear Purple* (Papier-Mache Press, 1987); *Pass/Fail: 32 Stories About Teaching* (Red Sky Books, 2001); and *Voices From the Couch* (America House, 2001). An excerpt from *Faulkner & Friends* appeared in the anthology *Umpteen Ways of Looking at a Possum: Critical* and *Creative Responses to Everette Maddox* (Xavier Review Press, 2006). She holds an MFA in creative writing from Louisiana State University in Baton Rouge.

Faulkner & Friends

CPSIA information can be obtained at www.ICGtesting.com
Printed in the USA
LVOW04s2253120914

403767LV00003B/3/P